STARBOUND

STEALING THE SUN
BOOK 4

RON COLLINS

SKYFOX PUBLISHING
Science Fiction

STARBOUND

STEALING THE SUN: BOOK 5

Skyfox Publishing

ISBN-10: 1-946176-08-7
ISBN-13: 978-1-946176-08-0

For Lisa.

Thanks!

The fault is not in our stars, but in ourselves

William Shakespeare

INTRODUCTION

When I was working on my fantasy serial, *Saga of the God-Touched Mage*, I had envisioned seven books. When I got to the end of book seven, however, I was not happy. It didn't feel "finished." But I plodded along in the development and production phase until one day I was taking a walk and realized why the story didn't feel finished.

My wife, who is a brilliant copyeditor, and my daughter, who is a brilliant writer, made appropriate fun of my obliviousness, then I proceeded to write the eighth and final volume. When that was finished I knew that yes, the story was done.

You know where this is going, right?

Yes, this is a long way of saying that the book you have in your hands was not supposed to exist.

At least not as a stand-alone book.

The original plan was for the series to be complete in five volumes. The storyline that fits in right here was going to be the end of *Starclash*, which, if you're following along like I know you are, is book four. The fates, however, have a fine sense of humor. The storylines didn't fit together right if I kept them together. So once again I expanded a series by one book, and, in the end, added what turned out to be about half the material in this book in order to tell the story it wanted to tell.

When I told Brigid (my daughter) of my need to add a book, she said something wise like "this is getting to be a habit for you, isn't it?"

So, yeah.

Sorry about that.

This is how my creative process goes, though.

Some people apparently just sit down, start at the beginning, and write along blissfully until they get to the end. Then they are done. I believe it was Anne Lamott who said we don't like those people very much, which is not completely true except to the extent that it is true. On the bad days anyway. We are allowed to be just the littlest bit jealous of those people on the bad days, aren't we?

I, however, work differently.

I sit down and I write and I go along path A until path A makes me bored or feels wrong, and then I go down Path B. Unless I plot things out—in which case I follow the plot until *it* makes me bored or until, more likely, some new shiny idea flutters its eyelashes at me and I'm off running in another direction.

Or, sometimes I get a cool idea that bubbles into a scene and sits there for three weeks until something else bubbles up later that tells me it's related to that first idea in ways I would never have guessed.

Or, I write on something until I can't stand it and I just toss the whole damned thing away to start something else.

Yes, I throw away a lot of words. Sometimes thousands at a time. (Aside: I once met a writer who said he kept everything he wrote— every snippet, every idea, every phrase, because he never knew when it might become useful. I believe him, I suppose. But I am not that kind of writer. I am not that organized. If I did that, I would never be able to find these things, anyway.)

The reason I'm telling you this now is that there was a time when I was afraid to throw away words, or afraid to make changes in midcourse. I figured those words were my investment, and that tossing them was akin to losing that investment. I thought that once I started in a direction, I should plow ahead until I got wherever I was going.

This isn't true, of course. In fact, it's dangerous for a writer like me. But it takes a certain level of courage to throw away things that aren't working, and it takes a sense of humility to go back and change course.

I think about that a lot right now.

This entire set of books is really about humanity and how it looks at itself—how it struggles to deal with conflict within itself and how that conflict makes it easy to miss the wonders of life that are happening all around us.

The characters are (I hope) striving to figure out who they are amid a backdrop of people who exert disproportionate influence on people's lives merely because they find themselves able to make decisions from behind the cover of a government or a company or…whatever.

Their world is strange.

They feel pulled.

They feel defenseless, or powerful.

If I've done my job well, you'll think they are all working hard to achieve their own goals, goals they all think of as worthy.

And yet, sometimes things go all to hell.

Sound familiar?

Maybe this is why I'm thinking about restarts.

Thinking about resets.

Thinking about throwing away words that aren't working and going back to a certain waypoint to start all over again.

Ron Collins
February 2017

NEWS

SOURCE: INFOWAVE — NEWS for the 23rd century
TRANSMITTED: August 20, 2215, Earth Standard
HEADLINE: Star Drive Program Termed "Military Priority"

Less than a week after Universe Three's surprise attack on Venus Station, Press Secretary Ophelia Nichols met with reporters to outline steps United Government Interstellar Command will take to gather control of the Star Drive program.

She announced that two Excelsior class spacecraft originally intended to support missions with tourist and commercial appeal will be diverted to military applications. In addition, Magellan, a ship expected to send scientists to remote star systems in order to better understand the origin of life, among other questions, will be delayed by as much as six standard months.

"We take this action, fully understanding it will set back our efforts in scientific research," Nichols said. "But the United Government is always going to err on the side of protecting its people."

SOURCE: INFOWAVE — NEWS for the 23rd century
TRANSMITTED: September 1, 2215, Earth Standard
HEADLINE: Students Killed in Freak Accident

Four Solar Academy students were killed when the lunar skimmer they modified failed. Friends of the students said they were secretly working on a micro Star Drive spacecraft to win the Academy's annual Engineers Day competition. Authorities are not releasing information on the cause of the accident, but sources close to the students have said their covert link to Alpha Centauri A's flow of fusion material apparently worked, but that the multidimensional deflection shield that Star Drive crafts deploy when racing at speeds greater than light failed during a test run.

The names of the four victims are being withheld pending notification of their families.

SETTING PRIORITIES

CHAPTER 1

Europa Station: Jovian Science Center
Local Date: September 3, 2215
Local Time: 1420

Watching technical people debate, while sometimes entertaining, was never particularly fun.

It could have been worse, Torrance Black thought as he wiped his clammy palms down his pants while the scientists argued. *They could have cancelled* Magellan *completely.*

Twenty-two years of service had given him plenty of practice dealing with tension that came from powerful people. Admirals, after all, were about the line of stars that ran across their collars, and subordinates followed a captain because, competent or not, a captain on the warpath had free rein to screw up your day. Add to this the fact that Torrance's current job in the UG's ambassadorial office—officially, the United Government Science Ambassador to Europa Station—reported into the murky hierarchy of the Office of Coordination (UGOC) and meant his command chain wove an awkward path through the leadership structures of every space station and ground-based province in the Solar System. As such, Torrance was learning the joys of dealing with a freewheeling network of egomaniacs, all of whom understood how to shovel more than their share of discomfort.

This situation was different, however.

Today he was sitting in a large conference center of brilliant scientists, ultracompetent mission planners, and several other professionals whose minds ran like they were stuck on faster-than-light. The chatter of the translation bug he had in his ear was filled with conversation, and the sense of anticipation he got from sitting with some of the biggest names known to research academia gave everything a sharp sense of being that was hard to duplicate.

Supreme President Laney Mubadid's directive meant UGIS *Magellan*, the first Excelsior class Star Drive spacecraft that was intended for the scientific exploration of the galaxy, would still roll off the production line in less than a year. The idea that such a ship was being built in the middle of what had every appearance of a long-running war with Universe Three stood testament to Ambassador Alberto Reyes's political connections. Reyes was Torrance's mentor, and the main reason he had a front-row ticket to the event. The opportunity to be a part of this kind of science made Torrance feel like a kid discovering Santa Claus was real.

They were going to the stars for science.

Actually planning missions that would bring hands-on data about the galaxy they lived in back to the Solar System, which was the conclave's purpose—develop a priority list for what to do and when to do it.

The fundamental engineering it took to run a spacecraft's system commands was embarrassingly basic relative to this kind of problem, and being with this crowd meant Torrance felt clumsy, so far out of his league that he could barely function. So, while the heightened awareness that prickled his neck today matched the pressure that came with a CO's scrutiny, this anxiety was both deeper and more personal.

It didn't help that Torrance had a personal stake in the matter, and that he knew he was fighting for a cause that went against the grain.

Life would be so much simpler if the people in charge of things would just do what he wanted them to do.

However…

His thumb pressed against the memory crystal he kept in his pocket. Data from Eden, of course. The edge of the block was solid against his skin. Even if he wasn't actively digging through it anymore, having the cube with him gave him comfort, and he needed every bit of support he could get today. As he pressed against the crystal, Torrance felt desire as strong as anything he had ever felt. He wanted to put a return trip to the Alpha Centauri system onto the slate. He wanted to study the planets around Alpha Centauri A—specifically Eden. It was all he had been able to think about since the day Reyes had informed him of the session.

Torrance's call beacon flared.

"You have been quiet, Ambassador Black." It was Tia Lark, executive director of the lab's astrobiology center, and a woman who had been given control of the exploratory council—her first assignment with such prestige. "Do you have recommendations or guidance from the UGOC?"

Torrance cleared his throat and recited a practiced line.

"The Office of Coordination understands that our first priority will always be the war effort," Torrance replied.

"As is ours," Lark replied as her role demanded.

"After gathering requests and feedback from all constituencies, we do, however, consider two items to be of the greatest value to our society's growth in the future."

"Two?"

The expression on Lark's face told him she understood that the second was his own agenda, but her voice remained steady and professional. It was not beyond most politicians to bring their own voices to such data, and Torrance had to admit that his role now made him a politician like the rest of them.

"Yes," he replied. "Two."

"And those would be?"

"Pi Mensae is known to have three planets in habitable regions, as well as a far-orbit planet of pure ice. The Office of Coordination considers it to be a prime area for early human expansion."

"Yes," Lark replied. "Pi M is a potential target. The star itself is larger than Sol, and appears to be heavy. But as you've seen, it scores lower on decision metrics due to uncertainty that the planets in the habitable zones will carry enough water."

"It's the heaviness that has the OC most interested," Torrance admitted. "And the ice planets local to the system could easily be harvested if necessary."

This time, Lark was less successful in masking the distaste on her expression.

Heavy was a term that meant the star was comprised of more metals than others. *Light*, of course, meant the opposite—a star with limited metallicity. Heavy systems meant more materials for building would be found among the system's planets. It also meant more materials for mining, more materials for trade. Or, to be exact, a heavy system meant more money. In Pi Mensae's case, the UG's interest in the system was all about iron—every industrialist in the Solar System wanted a piece of the action.

"The argument for Pi Mensae is already understood," Lark said. "And those arguments will be debated over the next several days. But I note the UGOC's interest in the project and will include its recommendation into the record." She paused for the recorder to make its annotation. "What is the Office of Coordination's second consideration?"

Torrance swallowed his anxiety.

"An element of our office suggests a return to the Alpha Centauri system to study the effects of our use of the source wormhole gate on the ecosystem of planets that lie within."

"That's absurd," Fredric Parson said.

Conversation came to an awkward halt.

Dr. Parson was an old man by most measures, having famously been in the initial groups of people who underwent telomere therapy to extend his years, but he still carried a huge reputation. He had been a leading figure in the development of the earliest wormhole models, and it was well known that Kransky, of the famous Kransky-Watt duo who eventually published the physics of wormhole technology, wouldn't have gotten as far as he had if Parson hadn't first solved the riddle of negative mass. In this way, Fredric Parson was, perhaps, the true father of the wormhole.

"Why is that," Lark replied.

Parson rose with an awkward lurch.

"The wormhole gate will have no effect on the Alpha Centauri system because the Alpha Centauri system is already dead. Far better to spend our resources understanding places that matter."

"With all due respect," Torrance replied. "Even if the Alpha Centauri planets are dead—a fact that we don't actually know for certain—there is still valuable science to run regarding the impact we are creating by burning up a star. To properly study this, we should plan multiple trips to the system, spaced years apart."

"The answer to those questions are not pressing, and the existence of Star Drives themselves means we have plenty of time for that work when it becomes valuable," Parson said. "Our current star will last centuries, even with Universe Three's warcraft burning through it like they are drunk kids in college."

Lark broke in. "I concur. And I note for the record that we've already come to consensus on the view that it will be most valuable to focus our recommendations on planets we know can harbor life."

Murmurs of agreement came from around the room as the translations completed. An impatient cough rang out from a back corner.

"The planets in the Alpha Centauri system could still harbor life," Torrance said.

"Not likely," Parson retorted. "Do you know how long we've been tabulating a catalog of planets with habitable biomarkers? We have, um, more than a few. Eden is not on that list."

"Eden has O2 signatures."

"Yes, but it also has sulfur and no water."

"Limited water," Torrance snapped back.

"Not enough to rank in the top 100 prospects. Probably not the top 500."

"It's number 752 by the Denning Method," another person added.

Torrance fought a grimace.

The Denning Method of ranking habitable planets was created

years prior by a gathering of scientists led by Clare Denning, a professor at Canyon Cave University, an institute in Arizona. It clearly did not score Eden well.

"There is still relevant science to do there," Torrance argued. "For example, if there is oxygen resident on the planet, why is it dying? Or maybe it's on a growth cycle."

"Look, Torrance," Parson said in a voice that said he had lost what little patience he might have started with. "We all know this is your pet project, but you can't be serious. I mean, that kind of science isn't even a simple jump run. A full scan of a planet that's likely poisonous requires a landing team and all the logistics and long-term support that such a team would need to survive."

"That is a very high cost," Lark added.

"There are much better options," Parson said.

Heat rose in Torrance's cheeks.

He was going to lose.

That much had been obvious from the beginning, but Parson's categorization of the effort as something everyone knew of as his personal pet project made it clear Torrance had crossed the line from "finished" to "treading on ground littered with pits of career quicksand."

How much of his reputation was he willing to lose?

A wave of despair dug at his gut.

He *was* a hero, after all.

Torrance had saved hundreds of people on *Everguard*, and his performance on *Orion* had been critical to the courts-martial of several military personnel who had gone rogue, killed Universe Three's charismatic leader, and effectively triggered the full-blown interstellar war with the U3 terrorists.

He understood how this worked, though.

If he clung to this position, everyone here would say he was an ideological quack. They would say he couldn't see the world through anything other than his own lens. In this world, where the act of having an open mind was a blood sport, the ability to at least pretend to change their opinions carried a certain cachet.

If he stuck to his guns, the people here would stop working with him. He would be just another old military guy trying to milk his past record, and his career would soon be filed under *What have you done for me lately?*

"You're right, Fredric," Torrance said. "I apologize for taking such time from the agenda."

"Thank you, Ambassador," Lark said. Her smile showed the relief of not having to proceed down a disciplinary path. "Please let your OC controllers know we will table the idea, but leave it on the record for future consideration."

When the conversation moved on, he breathed his own sigh of relief.

His defeat sat like a rock in his gut.

He ran his fingers across the data cube again, and felt a now-familiar sense of loss.

A memory of the regret that seemed perpetually pasted onto his father's expression came over him then. And the way his father's voice would trail away in the few times that Torrance had been able to talk about the idea of dreams and the future. He hadn't thought of his dad for a while. Torrance's father had been born an optimist in general, but was hardened down by the passage of time and probably more than a few moments of bad luck. The thought lay on his mind like a sleepless night.

Unless you have a certain sense of power, Torrance thought, some things in this world are just not meant to be.

The exploration of Eden was among those things.

CHAPTER 2

Europa Station: Jovian Science Center
Local Date: September 5, 2215
Local Time: 1850

The hallways of the Jovian Science Center were wide and bright. A crispness in the air made Torrance think about the air handling system. It being late in the day, the corridors were also empty enough that Torrance could hear the tread of his footsteps against the soft composite that made up most of the station's flooring. The artificial gravity here was created by combining the rotational effects of the station itself with a state-of-the-art controller that allowed for personalized adjustments in the pull the system exerted on the atomic structure of each person. Torrance had his setting turned to something that made him feel like he was nearly floating.

He missed Systems Command, and realized then that he should have already checked in with the shipboard systems leader just to pay respects.

Torrance was tired now, though. His brain was numb. He felt beat down and still annoyingly restless about having failed to get his mission on the priority list. He pulled back his sleeve and scanned messages as he walked toward his office. Thirty minutes ago Tia Lark pounded the traditional gavel and brought the three-day debate to its end. Per protocol, he had turned off all personal channels during the session, so a backlog of chatter rolled over his system in a stream long enough to make his eyes go crossed.

At least the conference was finished and the decisions had been made—the scientists' part of the decisions, anyway.

Next, Lark would take the proposed mission list to her commission leaders. The business people would make their arguments, then the United Congresses would tear it down and build it up again for the supreme president's signature. But Torrance understood how this process would work now. The system would massage words and passages so that everyone could say they had a part in it. Certain things would be lost or dumbed down, but at the end of the day the list wouldn't change much. Politicians who went against the recommendations would be exposing themselves to ridicule if something went wrong. Beyond that, many of the scientists were in the pockets of businessmen who had various interests across the system anyway, so the list already had their interests baked into it. Other than the need to get their names on the operational papers, neither CEOs nor political leaders had much incentive to overwork the process.

Torrance drew near his office.

He planned to send a coded brief to Ambassador Reyes, then head back to quarters where Marisa would be up and cooking. Just the thought made his stomach throb. Lunch had been early and coffee had been often. The idea of Marisa pushing the limits of her recovery from the burns she received on *Everguard* made him smile, too. She had never cooked much before, but she was also never one to be able to sit still for long. As a result, where doctors had suggested years of recovery, Marisa was already up and working.

As he approached, the door opened.

He stepped into his office.

The overhead lights were off, but the soft glow from Jupiter streamed through a wide window and highlighted the silhouette of a man standing with his back to him.

Torrance drew up short.

Even before the man turned, it registered that he was young.

"LC," he said.

Torrance knew the voice immediately.

"Thomas!"

Now in his early twenties, Kitchell had found his height but still had room to fill in his lanky frame. When he put his hand out to shake, it levered forward with an awkward motion that made it seem like his arm was growing.

Torrance grabbed Kitchell's hand and shook it vigorously.

"I knew you were coming, but it's still a great surprise to see you. How did you manage to sneak into the office?"

"I pulled a bit of a string."

"Kulpani," Torrance said.

Given Torrance and Kitchell's history, the station's CEO and president would likely have authorized the kid to do about anything to surprise Torrance.

"I figured you would have just rejiggered the security system," Torrance said.

"Those days are behind me, I think."

"I suppose that's for the best."

Kitchell scanned the office. "Looks like you've managed a heck of an upgrade."

"Huh," Torrance replied. A satisfied grin spread over his face. "I hadn't noticed."

"I'm sure you didn't."

"Come have a seat," Torrance said, guiding Kitchell to the desk and chairs that filled the room opposite the observation window. "Let me get you something to drink. Have you had dinner?"

Kitchell waved his hand as he settled into a chair.

"Nothing to drink right now. I'm planning to do the Central Pavilion for dinner in a little bit. I've heard it's good."

"Marisa will kick my backside all the way to the ice fields if she hears I let you skip out on your first night. And there's nothing at the

Pavilion that's as good as what she's fixing up now. You can go some-where else tomorrow. I'll let her know you're coming."

Kitchell shrugged. "Yes, sir."

Torrance tapped a message. Marisa replied almost before he finished.

He smiled. "No ice fields for me."

"Good to hear."

The office seats were plastifoam, and amazingly comfortable. Still new enough to smell occasionally of their packaging. Their frames adjusted to the person who sat on them, and could be heated or cooled with a comment or the touch of a pad. The pentagonal desktop had an ultrahigh-resolution projector node embedded in each corner, each projector node direct-linked to Abke.

"Sweet system," Kitchell said, admiring the projector closest to him.

"Very edge," Torrance replied.

"That phrase is deader than a brown dwarf, LC."

Torrance gave a sheepish shrug. "Sometimes I tell the seats to heat up and cool down just because I can."

Kitchell continued his examination. "Five-D projection."

"Seems like a bit of an overkill, really. All I do with it is read reports."

"Kind of like using a wormhole jump to go from Earth to the moon," Kitchell said.

Torrance chuckled. "Couldn't have said it better myself. It would have been great back when we were on *Everguard*," he said.

Torrance glanced around the office while Kitchell finished his own examination. He realized then that he had already begun to take for granted the observation shell that rolled back from the window when-ever the station's position allowed the hardened windows to protect against Jupiter's radiation field.

All in all, this was a true executive's office.

He found himself, however, not wanting to tell Kitchell about the security features of the office that came with the title of ambassador.

"It's interesting how quickly the world around you can become mundane," Torrance said.

"You've come a long way."

Torrance nodded. "To be honest, I kind of miss being down in the bowels of *Everguard*."

"Once a systems guy, always a systems guy."

The two of them sat smiling for a fraction of a second too long.

"So you're here to intern," Torrance said. "We should probably come up with an assignment."

Kitchell's smile was nearly as luminous as Jupiter outside the window. He leaned back in his seat, and crossed his hands in front of his belly. "Already have one," he said.

Without conscious thought, Torrance felt the outline of the memory crystal in his pocket.

"You'll get creamed if you take on the project I think you're suggesting."

"Maybe," Kitchell said. "Maybe not."

The kid seemed to glow.

"What do you have up your sleeve?" Torrance said.

"It'll take a while to describe. Lieutenant Harthing might like it better if we talked about it tomorrow."

"Or over dinner?"

"As long as it won't bore her."

"Marisa is dying to hear something technical."

"Fair enough, then."

"Let's hit the boosters, then."

Torrance stood, and Kitchell followed.

He led them both out the door, which locked behind them.

It felt great to be with the kid again. Kitchell reeked of hopes and of dreams. Torrance's stride lengthened and smoothed out. The smell of the corridor seemed fresh now rather than merely clean.

They made small talk as Torrance led them through the academic wing, and into the station's spindle. Five minutes later, a lift tube deposited them in the zone of private quarters.

Marisa would be waiting.

It wasn't until the next day that Torrance realized he hadn't sent Reyes his initial report on the conference.

CHAPTER 3

Europa Station: Jovian Science Center
Local Date: September 5, 2215
Local Time: 1930

"It's a new piece of math," Kitchell said after he took a bite of the bruschetta Marisa put on a plate before him. "It basically comes from cryptograph folks who were looking for ways to hide information."

"Leave it to the spooks, right?" Torrance replied.

Marisa sat down across from Torrance, with Kitchell to her left.

Her hair was growing back, but was still short. The scarring on her face was obvious, but Torrance knew the skin on the rest of her body was worse. She was embarrassed by the pity other people directed her way because of her scars. It was a medical miracle that Marisa Harthing had survived her burns at all, and a testament to the nursing professions that she had recovered as well as she had. The regrowth of skin had been painful to watch, and almost certainly unbearable to experience.

He wondered how the experience would change her in the long run.

"This bruschetta is fantastic," the younger man said to Marisa.

The bruschetta was perfectly grilled and covered in a mix of cheese, garlic, and oils that created a gloriously rich sensation that rolled all the way through Torrance's body. He hadn't realized he was so hungry.

"Thank you," she replied, covering the side of her face as she gave an involuntary smile.

Dinner was linguine and a meat sauce. Kitchell opted for beer, but Marisa and Torrance shared a red wine blend. Kitchell raised a fork in preparation of attacking the linguine.

"How are you doing?" he asked her.

Torrance liked the kid's direct manner. It seemed to him that Kitchell had been born with some kind of internal marker that let him understand other people. When the boy was a kid, he used that compass to help him dig under people's skin, but now that he had grown up he was turning the skill to more useful pursuits. Today Kitchell's directness and matter-of-fact tone combined to give the conversation a sense of safety that would help Marisa open up. Someday Kitchell was going to make a brilliant mentor.

"I'm good," she replied. "Really just trying to get my energy up to normal."

"After her stamina comes back, Marisa is going to have bot-surgery and genetic reconstruction to do a complete reset of her skin," Torrance said.

"Ouch," Kitchell replied.

She shrugged and ate linguine. "Pretty good if I say so myself."

"You can," Kitchell said.

"Maybe more rosemary next time," she replied.

"I've heard skin regen is painful," Kitchell said.

Marisa chewed. Her eyes got a distant expression, and she took a breath. "Can't be much worse than what's already happened."

"It will get rid of the scarring," Torrance said. "And it will be a stronger barrier to disease than she has now. It's amazing how complex your skin is."

"When will you be done?" Kitchell looked at Marisa.

"Depends. Could be months. The doctor says a lot depends on me, so I'm trying to get active again."

"PT every day," Torrance said. "Even if it's just for a few minutes."

Kitchell's face took on the expression of a son asking what Torrance's intentions were toward his mother—which was a helluva big question right now. Torrance and Marisa had dated on *Everguard,* but Torrance screwed that up and then their career goals seemed to be so divergent it hadn't made sense to be anything but friends. Then came the attack and Marisa's injury, and the opportunity to help her. All Torrance could say right now was that he admired the hell out of her. But until the past few weeks, the entire thrust of their new relationship had been focused so intensely on getting her back on her feet that there hadn't been time, opportunity, or even reason to think about that kind of question.

At least that was his excuse.

Now that she was getting back to being herself, Torrance didn't know how she really felt about him anymore. He had wanted to talk about it, but the idea scared him. What if she didn't want to stay? He had been looking out after her for over six months now. It was a long grind, really. At first he had known how self-serving his diligence had been, that his caring for her had come from a guilty place. He had been the one who ordered her to cover Rear Deck, so her injuries were on him.

Somewhere along the line, though, that sense of duty wore away.

Now he was here because he loved Marisa.

Or did he?

Life was confusing as hell sometimes. All he could say for sure was that he liked being with Marisa. She made him happy.

He ate linguine and bruschetta as he let the question on Kitchell's gaze fade away.

"Tell me about this new math," he said.

Kitchell took the bait.

"Technically I guess it's not so much new math as it is applying recently developed stuff to different problems," he said. "I got the base idea from one of the professors at the Academy. He was laying out concepts he got after hearing that the intelligence wonks were playing with a quantum mechanical crypto technique that strips patterns from sources in multiple cycles," Kitchell said. "Simplifying things greatly, the idea is that each source leaves unique garbage information buried inside the atomic structure of whatever laminate gets used to store the data."

"Interesting," Torrance said.

"If you can find those patterns, you stand a better than reasonable chance to reconstruct the root data that carried them."

"Even more interesting," Torrance said. He had heard about some of this earlier when he had checked up on Kitchell's progress, but the theory behind the use of this technique was more than a bit beyond him. He had intended to follow up, but that was more from a professional curiosity than anything else, and it had been a very low priority.

"It is interesting, isn't it?"

The kid's voice was getting that flavor of excitement on it.

He continued. "I don't pretend to understand everything the intelligence guys are doing right now, but from a simple signal processing perspective it all adds up to the idea that if you can separate out various signals hiding in a blob, you could pass communication off by laying dirty messages over top of the ones you want someone to find."

"Then the receiver reads the message by removing layers?" Marisa replied.

Kitchell nodded, sipping beer. "Which is easy if you know the patterns that need to be removed and the order you need to remove them in. But it gets grossly complex if you don't know both of those things."

Understanding began to dawn on Torrance.

"Something tells me that the next thing you're going to say is that you have a way to strip layers away even if you don't know the patterns or the order."

Kitchell's eyes glistened and his cheeks colored.

"It takes massive computing power, but I think so. At least I've got a theory for a theory."

Torrance waited.

"Mostly it's about digging into the atomic structure of the laminate to look at the garbage the process leaves behind. You look for crosstalk in the lattice, cross-patterns. It's kind of like reading a beach you're walking on. You see patterns in the sand and use the idea of what a wave is to help reconstruct the wave itself. Then doing that for wave after wave so you can reconstruct one that rolled up the shore ten minutes ago."

"What you're saying," Torrance said, "is that you have an algorithm that finds patterns that don't actually exist?"

"No, that's what human beings do. This system would find and then rebuild patterns that would be there if other patterns weren't contaminating the original."

"You want to run the Eden data through your process," Torrance said.

"Almost."

Torrance gave Kitchell an annoyed glare.

"I mean, yes, I want to use the Eden data. I've already played with it a little, but we both know that data has problems—it's incomplete, and the resolution of its storage isn't as good as it could have been. Beyond that, if we're right about the idea of an embedded source, the patterns weren't layered so much as merged. Those are big problems for me right now."

Kitchell glanced at Marisa, then back to Torrance.

"So I want to work on a process that applies the method in a different way."

"Which is?" Torrance said.

"I want to merge my concept with artificial learning techniques so that the processing algorithm can adjust itself on each pass. I want to start with what is originally somewhat random patches of noise in a rapid-fire sequence to see what happens."

"You want to create an automated cipher," Torrance said.

Kitchell grinned, and immediately turned into a version of the brash teenager Torrance had first met.

"That's why you came here, right?" Torrance said. "You're looking for a quiet, off-the-record place where you can create a process to break the newest crypto the intelligence community is creating."

"I wouldn't put it that way."

"But that's how they would see it?"

"I don't understand," Marisa said, setting her fork down.

Torrance answered. "If Thomas can back out all the crap—if he can erase what are essentially random noise patterns to find language embedded below, he's essentially broken their code. If Thomas succeeds, he'll be able to read messages without knowing the original patterns."

"Is that true?" She looked at Kitchell.

He let his eyes grow wide in an expression of mock innocence.

"That's ballsy," Marisa said. "Especially for a first-year."

Kitchell raised his eyebrows.

"My advisers say I'm well beyond the average freshie."

"I can imagine."

That was no lie, Torrance thought. He could imagine a lot when it came to Thomas Kitchell. The boy had always been this weird combination of likeably capable and annoyingly clever.

"Will you help me?" Kitchell said. "I've already done a few runs with Eden's data, and despite all the problems the results are interesting enough. And the Eden files *are* the exact kind of information I need to work with. I know it's touchy, but in reality, since no one in the intel offices cares about these files I doubt anyone will really be watching me at all. Most likely anyone who learns about what I'm doing will just think I'm wasting time."

Torrance rubbed his eyes.

He was in this strange double-state where his brain was jumping on overdrive, but his body felt like so much dead wood.

"If you find anything, then what?"

"Then you have the data you need to win the argument for a trip back to Alpha Centauri A."

"No landing team," Marisa said, sipping her wine. "If you can read the data remotely, you don't have to create a mission that requires people to put boots planetside."

"That's right," Kitchell said.

Torrance saw it then, too.

If Kitchell could crack the code even just enough to prove there was a code, then Torrance could make a new argument. The idea burned in his mind and made him suddenly able to access that tiny edge of hope he had clung to for so long. After all this time, that sensation cut two ways, but it was still there. Thomas Kitchell was sitting here, giving him exactly what he needed to keep going after three days of disappointment.

Torrance reached for his wineglass, then looked at his dinner mates.

"Yes," Torrance finally said. "We'll need to be careful about how we progress on this, but I'll help you." He raised the liquid, sweet and red. "I think this calls for a toast, eh?"

The three touched glasses, and Torrance took a full mouthful. The robust layers of the red blend filled his mind.

If Kitchell was right, Torrance might just get his mission after all.

CHAPTER 4

Europa Station: Jovian Science Center
Local Date: January 7, 2216
Local Time: 1350

The news sat on Torrance's projection device.

SOURCE: INFOWAVE — NEWS for the 23rd century
TRANSMITTED: January 5, 2216, Earth Standard
HEADLINE: U3 Attack Repelled Over Asia, Over 300 Dead

Universe Three fire bombers flew in the skies over the rice fields of China district today, but damage was minimized due to antiair satellite cover and scrambled aircraft out of Hong Kong. In addition, the United Government's new Star Drive craft UGIS Venture arrived nearly immediately, and appar-

ently served to preempt the U3 attack patterns. At least 312 people are known killed, hundreds more wounded. The rice crop is reported to remain safe, though numbers were not released.

"We're angry," said district mayor Kenji Liu. "This attack is senseless. So many people dead."

Admiral Naomi Umaro, newly promoted to a UG staff position, had stronger words. "Universe Three has the ability to stop this war all by themselves. Or they could fight the thing honorably. Instead, they purposefully choose to fly these kinds of sorties against defenseless farmers."

The attack is the latest in a series of operations that U3 Leader Deidra Francis has threatened to execute against targets on Earth. "We will show the United Government," she said in a recently broadcast bulletin, "that as long as they continue to threaten our freedom, there is no safe place in the universe. That includes the mother planet."

His gut clenched as he scanned the report. It continued for paragraph after paragraph, conveying a litany of personal stories. The only positive note in the whole thing was that the damage done was less than earlier attacks U3 had pulled off.

This war was getting tougher to deal with every month.

Deidra Francis appeared to be no less adroit than her father, and she had an "advantage" in that she wasn't afraid to use force—or, at least she wasn't as constrained by the politics of the day as her father had been. Something told Torrance that Casmir Francis would have been just as bloodthirsty if it came down to it, but Francis, the elder, had been playing a game with peaceful recognition of Universe Three as a final target, whereas his daughter took the reins after that goal was no longer a reasonable expectation.

Torrance had already read the internal reports that came from the intelligence branch, so he understood more of the minutia than was written here, but the core was easy to follow, as was the response that would invariably come from the people and their UG leaders.

Now was not the time to dwell on this, though.

Difficult as it was, now was the time to prepare.

Jared Kulpani, the Jovian Science Center's president and CEO, was going to visit in ten minutes.

Torrance slid the report away, and dug back into his notes regarding Thomas Kitchell's findings.

The kid was truly brilliant.

War or no war, Torrance had to be ready.

———

Right on time, the door chimed and slid open.

Jared Kulpani stepped in, dressed as usual in sharply creased business attire and striding with the graceful movements of an athlete. In his late thirties, Kulpani was tall, with chiseled looks that attracted attention whenever he appeared anywhere. He was sharp-witted and quick on his feet, a man who had won pretty much every part of life's lottery but who also took advantage of those traits with hard work and intelligent application of every resource he was given. As the station's president, Kulpani was its ranking civilian officer.

Torrance rose and came around his desk.

"Ambassador Black," Kulpani said as he approached Torrance's desk. His smile was warm.

"Thank you for taking the inconvenience of coming here," Torrance replied, clasping Kulpani's hand.

"It was not an inconvenience at all. I was already attending a meeting in the science wing. No reason to make you venture out when you're right on my way."

Torrance nodded. The comment made sense when stacked up against Kulpani's reputation. The president and CEO was known to be all about efficiency, even when it came to his own behaviors. It was something Torrance admired about him. Most politicians saw efficiency as something they wanted from other people, but wouldn't understand how to put it into action themselves if their lives depended on it.

They took seats.

"Getting straight to it," Torrance said. "I want to present some research that Thomas Kitchell has done while interning for me the past few months."

"Yes."

Torrance went through his pitch.

He described the algorithm, and its purpose. Its use of multidimensional pattern matching, and its reliance on quantum identifications. He recounted tweaks Kitchell had made over time as he played with the data.

Then he inserted conversation about the Eden files, spending most of the rest of his time on patterns that emerged in Kitchell's output, putting them up on the projector but being certain to highlight the fact that none matched linguistics mechanisms available to them.

"They're really quite beautiful, aren't they," he said.

"You were exploring Eden?" Kulpani replied.

"Only as a basic source."

"You know your reputation, right? You know how that's going to look?"

"I'm telling you, Thomas only used that dataset because he was aware of it, and because it fit the needs of his project. My name will not appear on any dissertation that gets written, and the results say he should be granted permission to continue."

"Are you suggesting these patterns mean something?"

"The fact that cohesive patterns seem to exist in the source data is, at best, a suggestion that the possibility of intelligent life existing there cannot be ruled out. But, I would tread very carefully on how such information is analyzed. I *am* aware of my reputation. I'm not saying we've found intelligent life."

Kulpani scanned the data projection. He asked to see several other slices, standing at one point to work with the data manually. After a bit, he sat back.

"What are you asking me to do?"

"I want you to support a request for a slot on the priority list for a jump to Alpha Centauri for a data collection effort to support Thomas Kitchell's work. Given this finding, the mission profile doesn't need to be extensive. Just a jump to gather fresh emissions with equipment that's actually set to record what we want to record, then jump back. If you backed the idea, I can work through other channels to acquire additional support."

"And, for this I get, what?"

"You mean, beyond possibly being among the people who can claim to have found intelligent life in the universe?" Torrance replied, grinning.

"Yes," Kulpani said, most definitely not grinning. "That is what I mean."

Torrance collected himself. "What do you want?"

"My commitment here is finished next year."

"I see," Torrance replied. "And do you have another position in mind for the future?"

"As much as I admire the scientific community, I'm thinking about pursuing something that would stretch me. Something more like managing the Mars civilizations."

It was a natural movement, Torrance thought. Control a space station, then move to a larger, land-based civilization. That Kulpani was thinking specifics probably meant he had at least one more move planned after that. Torrance took him in. The CEO and president's gaze was sharp and intense.

"I assume you play a mean game of chess," Torrance responded.

Kulpani's expression grew softer. "Poker is more my game."

"I can see that, too." Torrance leaned on his desk and focused on the issue. "I think I can help with your goals. I have trips planned to Mars and Kensington in the next month. And Ambassador Reyes has asked me to make several contacts Earthside that might be valuable to you, also. I would be happy to discuss your qualifications with all of them."

Kulpani pursed his lips and glanced at the data column again. "Your mission can't be too high on the list," he said. "Could be a year or two before it happens."

"Things take what they take."

"Then I'll be happy to put whatever weight I have to your effort."

Torrance did his best to restrain a surge of adrenaline. Reyes would be proud of him.

"Thank you," he said. "What can I do to help your effort now?"

"Write the pitch. Send it to me."

"Consider it done."

Kulpani gave a bright smile, then stood. "Please pass my congratulations to Mr. Kitchell."

Torrance rose, also, and the two shook hands.

"I was wondering if I might run another idea past you," Torrance said.

"Aggressive today, aren't you?" the station president said.

"One only gets so many audiences with you," Torrance replied. "It's about Lieutenant Harthing."

"I understand she's undergoing skin therapy, right?"

"That's right." As Torrance paused, the image of Marisa came to him, her body covered in the matted swathes of therapy strips rearranging her skin's molecules an atom at a time. It was an unpleasant process, applied three times a day. "She's still finishing the regimen, but it's coming along well enough now. She's past the most painful parts, at least, and her therapist is happy. Mentally she's been biting at the bit. I'm wondering if we can find a role for her that might give her the ability to contribute."

"She was in guidance previously, right?"

"Navigation, yes."

Kulpani nodded. "I'm not sure how grandly we need a navigation person here on Europa Station, but I know she's bright."

"Sharper than me," Torrance said without a hint of humblebrag.

"I'm sure we can find something appropriate. Have her arrange a session."

"Thank you."

As Kulpani left, the station's rotation triggered the observation window's automatic rollback sequence. Alone in his office, Torrance stepped to the window, folded his arms across his belly, and watched the view come open.

It was a cold world out there, he thought.

But sometimes, if you stuck with it and if you looked at the picture just right, it was really quite amazing.

"Abke," he said. "Patch me in to Lieutenant Harthing's line."

"Connecting," Abke replied.

They were going to celebrate this together, even if that celebration consisted of only a walk and dinner out. But if Marisa Harthing played her cards right, she was going to go dancing for the first time in a very long time.

CHAPTER 5

Europa Station: Jovian Science Center
Local Date: January 7, 2216
Local Time: 1800

Torrance sat across the table from Marisa. They were at the Ocean View, a high-end restaurant built on one of the highest points of the station and named ironically for the remarkable view of Europa that came from its upper tier. The dining area was dimly lit to provide for the view, but the room was wide and open. The rich aroma wafting from the kitchen, an invisible fog of seared meat and baked vegetables, would have been worth the price tag alone, but Torrance would have paid twice as much if he had known for sure how the night out would affect her.

She was radiant tonight.

In the restaurant's dim light, Torrance could barely make out the darker patches of Marisa's skin that still remained to be fully repaired. Her expression was light and full of wonder that he hadn't seen since the accident. Her eyes were bright.

As they waited for their drinks, Marisa gazed over the rugged surface of the moon. From here, Europa was a collage of visual sensations—smooth and reflective in patches, shattered and cracked in others. The northern "desert" was ground rough and looked like iced concrete. From the station's current position, light from Jupiter fell on a crescent of the tide-locked moon, leaving a majority of the surface barely visible and fading to black.

"What are you thinking?" he said.

"About the freshwater miners there." She pointed to a spidery network of facilities scattered over the lighted side of Europa's surface. "And the idea that we have fifty scientists down under the crust. I'm thinking about how they're doing. What they're testing. Are they happy with their choices?" She gave a lilting chuckle accompanied with a wry smile. "I'm wondering if they're warm."

The scientists she referred to were on Donnager II, a submerged laboratory the Jovian Science Center funded and monitored. It had been operating in the open seas under Europa's surface for a decade now, and was chartered to study rudimentary life-forms that could survive in harsh temperatures. The pod was mobile, but was currently tethered to the floor just down current from a large thermal vent that served as the cultural center for a community of phosphorus bacteria and several multicell algae and molds, cousins to those found on Earth. It was one of several high-profile projects the center ran.

Torrance smiled. "Those are good questions."

"They're making a difference," she said, turning back to Torrance. "They're living in one of the harshest places a human being can possibly live in, but they aren't letting that stop them."

"I guess life is like that," Torrance said, feeling the edge of the data crystal without actually touching it. He caught a hint of Kitchell's energy. The idea of seeing real data from a mission focused on Eden made him happy in a marvelous way.

"What do you mean?" Marisa said.

"Life fights for its place."

"Like Universe Three."

"And like us."

And like you, Torrance was going to add. He held up at the last moment, though. No reason to push things too far now. Better to just let her be who she was.

"It's good to see you interested in things again," he said.

Marisa pressed her lips together and regarded him more intensely than she had in a long while. "Why are you doing this?"

"Doing what?"

"Taking care of me," she said. "Why are you taking care of me?"

Heat rose in Torrance's cheeks. "Isn't wanting to see you get better reason enough?"

"At first I thought you were just feeling guilty. You've always been susceptible to that, you know? Feeling bad for things that aren't really your fault—and I mean that in a good way. Then as time went along and you kept it together for me I thought maybe you were just doing your duty. You know, leader who sent a subordinate to battle and all that?"

The automated drink service arrived and placed long-stemmed wineglasses on the heavy tablecloth. They sat pristinely empty for a moment until the system poured wine, then left the bottle wrapped in its chill sleeve. The liquid gave an aroma that hinted of dark cherry.

"I don't want to hurt you," Marisa continued, "but you know it can't keep going like this, right?"

"Like this?" Torrance said.

"I've got to do something. I'm bored out of my skull."

Torrance picked up his wineglass by the stem and gave it an absent twirl, then glanced out the observation panel to the mining facility on Europa. "Is that what you really mean?"

"I don't know," Marisa said. Her lips twisted in a way that said she was thinking. "I can't possibly just stay at home and be an ambassador's partner."

"Too sedentary of a life, I suppose."

"Unfortunately."

He put the glass down.

"Then I suppose it's a good thing I talked to Jared Kulpani about you earlier today."

"What do you mean?"

"When we talked about Thomas's work, I told him you might be interested in doing something while you finished your recovery."

Marisa's jaw went slack, but carried a subtle smile.

It was an expression he enjoyed.

She started to speak, but Torrance raised his hand.

"Short term, only," he said. "I'm guessing you'll want to look into other roles with Interstellar Command once you're released back to active duty, but for now I thought you might like to get your feet wet again by helping some of the teams here. At least get back into the game."

Marisa bit her lip then. The beginning of tears formed in the corners of her eyes.

This is the moment, he thought.

How did he feel? What did he want? These were easier questions to avoid than to answer, but if things were going to be different this time, it seemed obvious this was the moment he needed to be clear about what he wanted. He needed Marisa to know he would always be on her side.

"I notice you didn't say we couldn't be together at all."

She sipped her wine, seemed to get ready to reply, but then held her tongue. She put her glass down, and sighed in a way that he couldn't interpret.

"I don't want you to be an ambassador's partner, Marisa. But I want you in my life."

"How does that work?"

Torrance opened a palm, then closed his fist. "I don't have a clue."

"That doesn't leave for good odds."

"I don't think it's about odds. I think it's about decisions and actions and sheer desire to make things work. I think it's about love—whatever we decide that means."

"I see."

"I know you'll be doing something different soon, and I'm going to be working with Coordinations for however long that lasts, and then—with some luck—*Magellan* will roll off the line and I'll get to do something with Eden. Neither one of us can say where we'll be over the next several years. But I like being with you, and I think you're amazing. I'm willing to help you get anywhere you want to go, wherever that is."

Marisa glanced to the moon again.

"Long distance?" she replied.

"Maybe," he said. "Maybe not. We've got some time to figure all the details out, so if you're willing I'd like to try."

"All right," she said. She gripped his hand back. "Let's see what happens."

He smiled. "This," he said, leaning forward to take her hand, "may well go down as being the best day in my life."

ARMS RACE

CHAPTER 6

U3 Ship *Icarus*, Apogee orbit
Fourth Planet, 37 Geminorum System
Local Date: Undefined
Local Time: 1/8:15

Temporary or not, when Universe Three first came to the 37 Geminorum system, Deidra Francis had brooked no argument on the naming of their new home. If Ellyn Parker took Perigee as her alias due to a need to be as close to the truth as possible, Deidra wanted this ball of rock to be known as Apogee for its distance from anything resembling the United Government.

Others had suggested something less obvious, something that would let what remained of their people settle into a more normal life. But Deidra would have none of that.

"There is no longer such a thing as a normal life for us," she proclaimed. She had been upset at the time. She would remember that for the rest of her life: Not yet twenty-two standard years old, and in control of the leadership of a Universe Three organization Papa—her father—had spent his life creating, still reeling from the destruction of their home in the Eta Cass system, and she was addressing the fate of the people she commanded. Not surprising her blood was up.

"This situation isn't what we prefer," she continued. "It's not what we asked for. But it's what we've been given by a United Government that has no sense of what true freedom means. Every person in our ranks needs to understand and see that from this point forward, we will always be at war with the United Government. To forget that is as good as signing our own death warrants."

Deidra was no fool. She understood how people would see her— raw and inexperienced, someone who might well be in over her head. Her organization hung by a vulnerable thread. Universe Three was on the run, working to find a new home where they could hide away and lick their wounds while they got their feet under them again.

It was important that things go right.

She was busy all the time now, of course, but one of the reasons she let herself work around the clock was that any time she slowed down Deidra found the doubts that rose in the sudden quiet grew loud enough to be debilitating.

"Better to keep moving," Papa had explained to her once. "Keep moving, and you can forget how little control you really have."

Deidra needed the people of Universe Three to see her as capable. She needed them to follow her.

She got her way on the question of names, of course.

Their new home planet would be called Apogee, which made her happy.

The Uglies had no idea where the planet was, which made her even happier.

And, while the logisticians made short work of getting the colony settled and headed toward self-sufficiency, she was able to direct a series of brilliantly successful raids on Solar System targets.

"It's like a shooting fish in the barrel," Katriana Martinez, her mentor and now captain of *Vengeance*, told her after one operation.

Which made Deidra happier still.

———

Right now, though, Deidra and the rest of her bridge team on *Icarus* had seen the result of their last attack run—a mission targeted at industrial complexes in Earth's China district, a mission that should have been straightforward but clearly had not gone as planned. The room had gone quiet when the reports rolled in, though, silent and cold. A new UG ship had disrupted everything.

Skimmers had been lost.

The damage done to the UG had been slight.

The room felt tight, and Deidra thought she could hear the breath rasping in and out of the lungs of every worker on the deck.

"Damn it," she said. "What happened?"

"The reports I have are inconclusive so far, Director," a communications operator replied.

"Unacceptable," she snapped.

"Deidra?" The question came from Gregor Anderson, her father's chief adviser. He sat at the copilot's control station because it was the closest seat. He was an old man now, and seemed to be growing old three times faster than he had been before both his best friend and his son had been killed. His hair had gone from distinguished gray to fragile white, and the color of his face had changed from fleshy to pale.

It bothered her to see the depths of Anderson's grief on everything from his features to his posture. Deidra Francis had lost more than most in the UG double cross, but she had no time to mourn.

The tone of Anderson's voice matched the concern that colored his face.

The comment was an admonition. He wanted her to be calm.

But screw him.

The sting of this defeat hurt.

"Sometimes a leader has to show what she's feeling," she said. "Even my father said that."

Anderson let his question hang.

The temperature of the room cooled even further.

She looked at the mission clock, which had just been synched to local time and which mostly served to annoy her that much further. She would never get used to a clock that started with what orbit the planet was on. That was the kind of thing that happens when your planet rotates in ten hours and your body deals in twenty-four-hour chunks, though. To make it more difficult, the planet completed an "annual" orbit in roughly forty-eight days, which had people whose lives were predicated on a calendar scrambling for options.

Life on Apogee was going to take some getting used to.

"Report from Captain Martinez," the comm officer said.

"Tell on," Deidra replied.

"It's marked confidential."

Deidra scanned the bridge. The faces were all turned her way. None of them would find it wrong for her to have the message sent to a briefing room, but that's not how she wanted to do this.

"If you're on this bridge, you've earned the right to hear what goes on here," she said aloud. "But what you hear is classified beyond that. Does everyone understand?"

Heads nodded.

"Tell on," she said to the communications officer.

"An unexpected Star Drive ship appeared in orbital space above China, Director," the man replied.

"I see," Deidra said, rubbing her eyes.

The mission profile called for *Vengeance*, Universe Three's second Star Drive spacecraft, to make a mess of China district then stop to gather the latest intel reports from moles in key positions across the Solar System. It *should* have been simple—get in, get out, no issues. But the intel was off.

"The UG has a new Star Drive?" It was Kazima Yamada, the U3's primary engineering coordinator, and the woman who was responsible for the implementation of technology and industrial capability as the colonization of Apogee proceeded.

"That's how I interpret it," Deidra replied.

"And I," Anderson said.

Deidra let the facts settle.

The Uglies had been ready, and they had a new ship themselves—which was ahead of schedule.

That was unacceptable.

"We have to have *Defender* ready now," Deidra said to Yamada.

Yamada scratched the back of her neck. The engineer's hair was beginning to go gray, but otherwise she could pass for a woman a decade younger than her fifty or more years. Fatigue showed in her face, though. The bugout from Atropos had her running on a serious lack of sleep.

"That's not going to happen, Deidra," Yamada said. "We've only been here two standard months. The facilities are just now taking shape."

"We need that ship now."

"It's not happening."

"You see the same thing we all see," Deidra argued. "Our advantage will be gone if we don't make this happen."

"We're doing our best to accelerate—"

"Our best isn't good enough."

The door to the bridge slid open, and Katriana Martinez stepped into the room. Her appearance turned heads, and made it clear that the rest of the room had remained awkwardly quiet during Deidra's argument with Yamada.

"Welcome home, Katriana," Deidra said.

If there was anyone in existence who could help calm Deidra, Martinez was that person. Katriana Martinez had been Deidra's mentor when they first came to Atropos. In many ways Deidra was closer to Martinez than she was to her mother.

"You have my report?" Martinez said.

"Yes," Deidra replied. "We've classified it for all coordinators, so speak freely."

"The United Government has accelerated their schedule. The intel we picked up from Miranda and on Kensington say that two more craft will be available mid-next Solar year."

Deidra turned to Yamada and raised an eyebrow that was more of a threat than anything else.

"Perhaps you need to find a new engineer," Yamada said. "I am already pushing everyone as hard as I can, Deidra. The system can only run as fast as practical."

Deidra rubbed one hand absently over the closed fist of her other hand.

"Kazima is right," Katriana said. "You cannot get blood from a beet."

"The people want vengeance," Deidra said.

"And they've had it," Anderson said. "Perhaps we should lay low for a brief respite."

"Lay low?" Deidra said.

"For a bit. The UG doesn't know where we are, so we could focus on putting everything we have behind engineering and construction. Give our crews a bit of a breather from the steady raids, and put our energy behind building a third ship faster."

Martinez nodded. "That could mean we could accelerate plans to spread over the system, too. We've been running raids every few day. I'm sure that's diverting a lot of attention."

Deidra, calming, took a breath, nodded.

"All right," she said. "I only have to be shouted down a few hundred times. We back off the raids, and we focus on building on Apogee. But I'm serious: Our only advantage is that we know where they are. I don't want to let the UG breathe. I want *Defender* as soon as is humanly possible."

"As do we all," Gregor said.

She turned to Yamada.

"What do you need?"

CHAPTER 7

Europa Station: Jovian Science Center
Local Date: March 14, 2217
Local Time: 1000

The last year had passed in the blink of an eye. *Magellan* would be ready for maiden voyage in three weeks. There were a million things to do.

Torrance sat in CEO and President Kulpani's waiting area, sipping coffee that Kulpani's steward had brought, and scanning information off the public projection system. Truth be told, it was nice to have a minute to himself.

The station's president and CEO had called him to a conference, which Torrance assumed was meant to ensure their basic pact hadn't been forgotten. Kulpani, as he had suggested before agreeing to help Torrance, would almost certainly not be the head of JSC this time next year, which, if all things went well, would be about the time the mission to Eden would roll up on the plan.

His days had been chock-full, listening to scientists work through plans for the initial jaunt to Eta Cassiopeia's Atropos, the long-ago abandoned home of Universe Three. The site was chosen as the initial target because Atropos's coordinates were items the UG was now intensely familiar with, and because the scientific community had data there that could be used as a baseline for calibrating their instrumentation.

The early priority list was full of what the community was calling "Jump and Bump" exercises—operations where *Magellan* would drop into a system, take a series of standard readings, then jump back. Given the time it took to re-gear the science required for each new mission, this profile meant the ship could run as many as fifty or so major excursions in a standard year—assuming, that is, that the jump coordinates were proven to be reliable.

It was a heady time to be the ambassador to JSC.

Other elements of the year had flown by, too.

Kitchell had finished his internship at JSC and returned to the Academy, where he was excelling.

Torrance and Marisa were doing well.

Marisa had stayed on site, and was logging fifteen-hour shifts with mathematicians at JSC's mapping lab, a group who were developing an all-out approach to use the UG's soon-to-be massive advantage in Star Drive ships to canvas the nearest star systems with intent to find Universe Three rebels and drive them out of whatever holes they were locked down in. The idea was to preprogram a series of jumps to cover more space in less time, but was severely limited by both physical stresses of the ship and crew, and the fact that no one knew the debris patterns inherent in any "fresh" star system. It was a complex problem, but one that, if mission planners could work out both the logistics of long-run jump exercises and the safety algorithms required to blind-hop, would be a major tactical advantage. It was one of those interesting technological developments that, like radar, sonar, and targeting theories of past history, could change the basic nature of war itself.

"It's interesting work," Marisa said late last night while she ate a warmed dinner in their quarters. "These people are all so brilliant, but none of them have ever actually been on a spacecraft that has to make all these moves they envision."

"Not unusual," Torrance said. "People are always discounting the difficulties of things they haven't done themselves."

"In this case, they aren't discounting so much as they're just naïve."

"They don't know what they don't know."

"Right."

"Like those kids who blew up their test spacecraft a couple years ago?"

"Yes, exactly. The news reports all focused on the fact that the kids got the math wrong, but the fact is that their jump actually worked for a moment. Their biggest error was that they jumped into space with too much debris and the ship disintegrated on arrival due to matter-energy conversion."

"Einstein wins again."

"Always does."

Torrance frowned. "So you've giving your bosses a perspective they haven't dealt with."

"You can say that again."

"So you're giving them—" Torrance stopped before Marisa tossed a couch pillow at him.

He caught it in midair, grinning.

Sitting at the end of the couch, legs curled under her, and holding her dinner plate in one hand and her fork raised in another, Marisa looked at Torrance and said, "What would you think about having a kid together?"

"What?"

"A kid. Together." She smiled then, clearly enjoying the perplexed expression on his face at her bombshell.

"But…," Torrance said, trying to process the idea, and at the same time trying to figure a way to politely remind Marisa that children were not an option for him.

"I've learned of a child on Europa who needs adopting," she said. "A little girl. I thought we might be able to help."

He had looked at her then, and saw what the question really meant. Raise a kid. Together.

Torrance was thinking about that when the door to the waiting area opened, and an unexpected man stepped in.

Torrance stood.

"Ambassador Reyes," he said. "This is a fantastic surprise."

Reyes was the reason he was in the Office of Coordination and, specifically, this position itself.

"Good to see you again, Torrance," Reyes replied, stepping forward to clasp his hand. The ambassador looked older than Torrance remembered him, the depth to the crevasses that ran down his face certainly deeper than his image on the projector chats had indicated. Torrance wondered how much adjusting Reyes had programed Abke to do.

The ambassador was dressed in the formal robes of the office, white upper flowing to bronze at the base, waist cinched with a sash tied to one side. A black shirt lay under the robe.

A woman came behind, also adorned as if from the upper regions of the Office of Coordination's hierarchy, but in addition wearing a thin chain around her neck that dangled over the shirt. She was as tall as Reyes, with dark hair. Younger than Reyes by at least a decade, probably two, maybe three.

"Ambassador Janic," Reyes said, turning to the woman, "please meet Ambassador Torrance Black." He squared himself with Torrance. "Ambassador Black, please greet Ambassador Farina Janic."

Torrance clasped her hand.

She was strong.

"I'm very glad to meet you, Torrance."

"Likewise. If I knew you were coming I would have—"

"Not a problem, Torrance," Reyes said. "Time didn't allow it, anyway."

"I understand that," Torrance said, though in truth he didn't. With a moment to reflect now, he wasn't sure what to think of this situation. "Please, have a seat," he said, motioning them to the other comfortable chairs arranged around the projection system. "I'm sure President Kulpani will want to see you, also."

"We have already seen Mr. Kulpani," Janic said. Her voice was as firm as her handshake.

Torrance sat back.

"This meeting was arranged for us by Mr. Kulpani, Torrance," Reyes said.

"I don't understand."

"I wanted to tell you personally."

"Tell me what?"

"First, that Farina here is going to take my place in the next cycle."

Torrance glanced to Ambassador Janic. "Congratulations."

"Thank you," she replied.

"And second?"

Ambassador Janic replied. "We wanted you to know that *Magellan*'s mission profile has been altered. She will no longer be a scientific vessel. Instead *Magellan* will be assigned to Interstellar Command, as will all other Star Drive spacecraft for the next two years."

A rock formed in Torrance's chest.

"Two years?" It was the most intelligent thing he could get out of his mouth at the time.

"Perhaps longer."

"I don't know what to say," Torrance replied. The months of work crashed down on him, and he rubbed his hands over his eyes. His face felt like rubber. He glanced at Reyes, knowing the energy the ambassador had put into his arrangements. "You negotiated this deal yourself. Can't you do anything?"

"I understand what *Magellan* meant to you, Torrance. But, as you are going to learn shortly, and as the general public will learn throughout the day as news reports are released, Universe Three has just flown missions with another new spacecraft of their own. The UG leadership's priorities are clear and their decisions have been made."

"Universe Three has their own production capability? Already?"

Janic's voice was hard this time. Firm and cold as Europa herself. "They are resourceful, Torrance. And they don't give up. You, of all people, should know what lengths they'll go to in order to defeat us."

"But they just bugged out of Atropos—"

"A very short while ago. True. All of it. But we've always known Universe Three was attempting to build a fleet, and they have to know we're going to dwarf their capacity soon, regardless. So it should come as no surprise that they've put everything they have into building this one."

Torrance's gaze bounced between Janic and Reyes.

He felt it then—the tension between the two.

At first Torrance had assumed Reyes was retiring or moving on, but he saw the truth now. Farina Janic had pushed the incumbent out. This was her play, and she had won. Alberto Reyes was on his farewell tour. Torrance wondered how much it had cost his mentor to allow him this one favor.

Janic spoke then. "I know I can count on you to serve the Office of Coordination in your usual fashion." The edge of her voice made the threat that rode under those words clear.

Reyes's expression carried resignation.

Torrance cleared his throat.

"Yes, Ambassador. I'm sure you can."

"Fantastic," she replied, then turned to Reyes. "In that case, we have more stops to make."

Reyes nodded. "I know you'll be busy making adjustments, Torrance. I hope you'll excuse us."

"Certainly, Ambassador," Torrance said.

Then they were gone, and Torrance Black found himself alone in CEO Kulpani's waiting room, staring at a column of yesterday's overly excited news releases that listed the many experiments that had been planned, but were now as empty as the holographic space the reports rode on.

Torrance drew a hard breath and shook his head.

He felt numb.

Lost.

Abandoned, powerless, and lied to, and…this was stupid. Idiotic.

Even with a third ship, Universe Three was no match for the UG—not for long, anyway. Everyone who actually thought about the situation would see that. Of course U3 was still finding ways to do damage to UG outposts with guerilla attacks, so he understood the danger. But that had almost nothing to do with the UG's space superiority. The issue was one of finding a needle in the proverbial cosmological haystack, and having one more military spacecraft wasn't going to do a damned thing to make that equation any better. To shut down all science projects for this kind of zero return was nothing but a political ploy.

It would work in that fashion, however, because people were afraid, and because people who were afraid would then vote to remove fear.

The fact was, however, that scientific advances had always resulted in advances to the public welfare. It wouldn't even surprise him if the slate of scientific operations they had planned would save lives of soldiers and pilots in the near term.

None of that mattered, though.

The program was all but dead.

Torrance sighed.

When his thoughts became semiclear again, he found his fist was clenched into a claw that held one of the throw cushions from Kulpani's couch.

He clenched his jaw tight, stood up, and threw the pillow hard across the room. The toss missed the porcelain statue that stood in the corner by a thin margin. Torrance found himself disquietingly upset that he missed.

Torrance collected himself then.

He straightened his jacket, and stepped away.

Reyes had been right. There was work to do, though to be honest Torrance had no idea what that work would be.

———

Later that night, Torrance received another call.

He had set his personal system on mute, so only now saw the call flag was flashing. He pulled himself from the review he was doing—trying to determine if he could salvage any projects by attaching them to military operations. The office was dark now, he noticed. The observation window had rotated closed earlier, and he was so caught up in his work he hadn't adjusted the lighting.

He checked the label and saw the message was from Marisa, then he checked the clock to see it was past seven o'clock local.

Shit.

He had said he would be home earlier.

"Return Marisa Harthing's call please, Abke."

"Connecting," Abke replied.

"Hello," Marisa said. "Oh, hi," she continued after apparently noting the source of the call. She sounded rushed.

"I'm sorry I'm running late," Torrance said.

The pause on the other side was slight, but still noticeable enough to be almost audible in itself.

"That means you haven't heard the news?"

"That *Magellan* is being reassigned? Yes, I've heard it."

"Not that news."

Torrance waited.

Marisa filled his silence. "I've been asked to be the Chief Navigation Officer on *Magellan*'s crew."

This time it was Torrance's hesitation that was audible.

"Isn't that amazing?" Marisa said.

"Yeah," Torrance replied. "Amazing. Totally amazing."

"I know it's late, so let's eat somewhere, all right?"

"Sure," Torrance said, looking at the time again.

"Ocean View?" Marisa said. "My treat."

He smiled at the joke they had been sharing for the past several months since they had started combining everything they did.

"Sounds great," he said. "But I'll make it my treat."

"Deal," she said, then disconnected.

For the second time today, Torrance sat alone, wondering what the hell had just happened.

CHAPTER 8

Apogee
Local Date: C2D10
Local Time: 2/9:45

I t was nighttime, but the "streets" were lit up by fire and the occasional celebratory rocket. Deidra sat on a rocky ledge of the hillside that looked down over the population of what they called a city, but in reality was just a small village. A few thousand people, really. Music played. The people were drinking.

The celebration made Deidra smile, despite herself.

Why not, she thought.

How many times does a group of people like this build one of the most complex pieces of machinery ever devised and do it in record time? And how often does a plan work exactly as it was drawn up? How many times does a raid result in total destruction of a military manufacturing base, without loss of even a single skimmer?

The night was hot and humid.

It was always hot here. Always humid.

To be honest, she hated Apogee.

She had come here to be alone. Thanks to the celebration, it was the first time she had been able to make that happen since the bugout, so many standard months ago. She thought about Kel and Jamal first, then her father. Matt Anderson. The rest of the people who had given so much for this success.

She thought about Ellyn Parker.

The three spheres of Universe Three.

She wondered about the future.

Brush rustled beside her.

She turned and brought her walking staff up to defend against a critter of some type, but saw her visitor was human.

Under cover of darkness, she allowed herself a grimace, but then saw the form of Katriana Martinez stepping toward her, a wine bottle in each hand.

"Hi," Deidra said.

If it would have been anyone else, Deidra would have told them to leave her alone. Instead, she just put her staff down.

Katriana was closer in age to Deidra's mother, than to Deidra. Her body was growing softer as she aged.

"Hi," Deidra said as she approached.

"Hola," Katriana replied as she proffered a bottle, then sat cross-legged beside Deidra.

The cork was gone, but the bottle was full.

Deidra took it and drank. The wine was still cool. It made her stomach feel good.

The two of them sat silently, watching the people of Universe Three party.

Deidre allowed her thoughts to return to Papa and Kel and Jamal. She drank more wine and remembered everyone she knew from before the United Government's double cross cost them Atropos.

"Today's victory was important," she said.

"Of course."

"Why does it feel so hollow?"

Katriana's smile was as thin as Deidra's comment. She raised the bottle to her lips and drank. Wine sloshed as she brought the bottle back down.

"I think it takes a long time to learn that all victories are temporary."

"I understand that."

"Do you?"

One side of Deidra's lips curled up. She gave a sheepish shrug. "I don't know."

"That's probably better."

The celebration continued. Deidra listened to a night creature sing in the distance.

"They are sitting ducks now," Deidra finally said.

"The Uglies?" Katriana replied.

The thickness of her tongue led Deidra to think Katriana had been drinking before she broke into this bottle—which was probably only fair. Her craft, *Vengeance*, and *Icarus* had been the decoys, flashing into the Solar System to draw the UG defenses while *Defender*, fresh off the line, wreaked havoc on the line of manufacturing plants that now dotted the Kensington Station line of asteroids.

"Yes, the Uglies."

Katriana nodded, her blond hair drooping over her face.

"Yes, they are," she said. "Barring some kind of screwup, we should be able to jump in and pick them off at will. For now, anyway."

Deidra nodded.

She didn't need Katriana to explain further.

This war was too far along to back out of, even if Deidra or the rest of Universe Three ever decided they wanted to.

The United Government wouldn't leave them alone now, and while Universe Three was going to be hard to find, it wasn't impossible to envision a future where the Uglies would discover their outpost. If that happened…

"I don't think we could survive that," Deidra said.

"They are very big," Katriana replied, then took a large swig of wine.

Yes, Deidra thought. Katriana Martinez had been drinking for some time.

"Maybe we should stop?" Deidra said.

"Stop attacking?"

"Yes."

"Bad idea."

"Why do you say that?"

Katriana used her free hand to wave at the celebration. "You see them, right?"

Deidra smiled.

"Besides, that's not who you are."

"I want to be like Ellyn and Papa."

"You think they would stop?"

Deidra hesitated. She had considered the question before, but now that Katriana was glaring at her, the answer was less clear.

When she was first deciding these courses of events and setting the U3 toward vengeance, Deidra worried that Gregor's accusations were right, that her own passions were hotter than those of the citizenry and that her desire for revenge for the death of her father was overwhelming her ability to lead the people. Gregor thought she was too young—as did several others. Admittedly, those concerns dimmed some time ago because, while many of the leadership group tried to stay with a message of peaceful freedom, it became clear to Deidra that the need for vengeance in their populace was high.

Nearly everyone she knew had lost someone to the UG.

And the fact was that both Ellyn Parker and Papa had come to understand that a certain degree of violence was necessary to make real change happen.

Neither Ellyn nor Papa would pull back now.

She was sure of that.

The UG was huge, though. They had billions of people, and what was essentially infinite resources relative to their own. Someday, something would happen, and the UG would find them.

The idea made her more tired than angry, more resigned than afraid.

No matter what happened going forward, this situation meant that she had to keep pressing the matter. UG was a monster, and U3 was an angered hornet that could attack as if from nowhere. If nothing else, every drop of blood they could draw from the beast drained it of resources it could use against them.

Aggression was now the ultimate form of defense.

She drank wine and listened to the music that filtered up from below. Drums and a stringed instrument. Katriana leaned against her, and the heat of her arm felt oddly good despite the heat of the night. For a moment Deidra imagined she could feel Kel's arm against hers. She recalled Kel's aroma, imagined the tone of her voice.

"You should find a man," Katriana said.

"Or a woman," Deidra responded. She didn't like this topic.

"Whichever."

Deidra smirked. "You've said that before."

"Don't wind up like me, Deidra. I live for the past. I let the world make me too hard, let my grief turn me cold."

"I like you just fine."

Katriana gave a gruff grunt.

"There is a way to stop this," Deidra said.

She glanced at Katriana, who nodded and gave a heavily lidded smile that told Deidra she had been deep into her own imaginings, likely a pair of little girls.

"A way to make it impossible for the UG to find us."

Katriana drew a deep breath and raised a skeptical eyebrow.

"If we can break the wormhole gate that fuels the Star Drives, they couldn't get to us," Deidra said. "And if that could happen, we would be free to live on our own."

A series of emotions went over Katriana's face then.

"Easier said than done, I think," she finally replied.

"Tomorrow I'm going to meet with Catazara and his scientists. We'll see what we can do."

Katriana raised her bottle to Deidra.

Deidra raised hers.

They drank, then. They watched the people of Universe Three party. They listened to their music.

Eventually, they went home.

CHAPTER 9

Europa Station: Jovian Science Center
Local Date: June 22, 2217
Local Time: 0945

Torrance looked at the listing he kept pinned in his projection system. Today would have been a launch day. Under the original plan, *Magellan* would already be posted in a spot in the TRAPPIST-1 system, and would jump to three additional locations assuming the safety scans Marisa's team worked out showed the landing zones could be managed.

Instead, there was no science happening outside the Solar System.

Instead, the only news worth scanning was a steady series of reports from the military wires as they jumped from rock to rock and achieved nothing more than reducing the possible locations of Universe Three outposts from ten billion to nine billion nine hundred ninety-nine million nine hundred ninety-nine thousand nine hundred ninety-nine.

That trickle of news seemed never-ending, but it would never be enough. In the meantime, Universe Three was running some kind of mission every week.

He thought about Marisa, stationed on *Magellan* and helping the ship hop through the galaxy on its classified mission path. All he could say about her whereabouts was that, assuming everything went as expected, she would return to the Solar System in a month. They would get a few weeks together, during which they would complete their adoption papers.

Then she would be gone again.

This would last at least two standard years, then she would likely move to another post.

"You have a call," Abke said.

He had missed his comm flag flashing. Abke's breaking into his thoughts meant the caller was on his "approved" list of priorities.

"Connect, please,' he said.

The image of Thomas Kitchell filled the screen.

"Thomas!"

"Hey, LC."

"Where are you?" The call was on standard channels and was nearly real time, so Kitchell had to be close by Europa Station.

"I'm on a shuttle, heading your way. Thought I would call to see if we could get together."

"That would be fantastic. What's the occasion?"

"I'm doing a research project for Professor Anders, and I need to work with a couple of the folks there. I'll only be on station for a few days."

"I can make myself free all week if you want," Torrance said, suddenly excited.

"All I've got is tonight."

Torrance tried to quiet his annoyance. He wanted to see Kitchell, and the idea that the kid would be on station but not want anything more than a simple check-in made him feel pitiful. Pining over the kid? Was that what his situation boiled down to now? The kid was a grown-up. He was making his own way. He didn't need the help of a washed-up ex-systems guy who spent his time shining the edges of missions that would probably never fly.

"One night is better than none," he said.

Kitchell gave one of those bright grins that only the young can manage.

"I'm sorry to hear about *Magellan*. I should have called earlier."

Torrance gave a now-practiced shrug. "Things work out as they work out."

"That might work on everyone else, but you can't hide your disappointment from me," Kitchell replied.

Torrance sat back.

"Seriously," Kitchell said. "I'm sure you're doing everything you can to get missions going. What can I do to help?"

"Nothing, Thomas. I love your enthusiasm. But you'll need to understand that once decisions have been made at a certain level, there's really nothing you can do to stop them."

"I can't accept that, LC. You and I both know we can't give up on Eden. Hell, the project I'm working on is focused on ideas about using multilayered composite data to process deep space radiation signals, but I'm doing it with the idea that the algorithms we create will have uses on the Eden data. There's got to be a way to get out there."

Torrance shook his head and scratched the back of his neck. The observation panel began to open, and he looked out to take in the pristinely rounded edge of Jupiter's profile. A wave of anger built inside him, sensations he had kept tightly bottled for months rising closer to the surface now in a dark and ugly surge.

"It doesn't matter," he said.

"It matters," Kitchell said. "Eden has your pod."

"Which, assuming they exist, will probably help them zero."

"Not true."

"Very true," Torrance snapped back.

When Kitchell didn't say anything, Torrance continued, his voice growing terser as he went.

"We both know this was a dumb-assed game from the beginning. Reengineering on that scale is damn well impossible. Too many things to go wrong, right? The pod itself has to make the surface, and then it has to stay in one piece. The civilization has to be there, and then has to actually see the damned thing. Just finding it could be near impossible, not to mention dealing with the technologies inside. Then, assuming these people have the math and science it takes just to figure out how it works, the pod would have to actually find those right 'people' to do it. Then there's manufacturing capability and the resources it takes to make spacefaring technology. What kind of metals they have on the planet, right? I mean, do you know how much molybdenum it takes to build a sensor system? Better yet all the other complex boxes it takes to build a spaceship? Christ. What kind of an idiot does it take to pretend that something like that could ever work?"

Torrance took a breath.

His fists were clenched even tighter than his jaws. He looked at Kitchell, who sat silently.

"I'm sorry," he said.

"Guess we should just quit, eh, LC?"

"That's where I'm at. I mean, crap. The fact that I'm mad about things doesn't make that entire argument wrong—and that doesn't even take into account the fact that even if there's an alien existence on Eden, it has to be at the right state of development to make anything happen."

"True."

They sat together for a bit.

"All of that discounts the one fact that matters, though, LC."

"What's that."

"That the life-forms on Eden have already proven they can send signals."

Torrance's chuckle was soft and full of mirth.

The kid's perseverance was annoying.

"Don't mind me, Thomas," he said. "I'm just…whatever."

"You're fed up. That's fine. I get that."

"The people who run this thing…they need to get a spine."

"They're too busy keeping themselves in their position," Kitchell replied. "Age-old game, right, LC? We've been through this before, right? You've said it time and time again. People argue among themselves about trivialities and ignore the things that are important, we drive our people into the ground in the name of protecting them, and we're willing to exterminate entire populations of creatures in the name of progress for ourselves. Does that do it?"

This time Torrance merely smirked, knowing what was coming.

"Yeah, I think that's got it."

"But, still, somehow we make things work."

Torrance pursed his lips.

"It's a long game, LC. If there's anything you've taught me over the years, it's that when you can't win today, fall back and play the long play. The truth eventually wins out."

"I hate that people have to pay the price, though."

"I know. That's why I think you're a helluva man."

Torrance sighed.

Kitchell was right about the long game.

Magellan may never take a scientific flight, but there would be other ships, and other moments. It would take time. Probably a lot of time. It meant the same battles would have to be fought again inside the scientific community, and then again in the political offices. With Farina Janic in Reyes's shoes, some of those battles might be more difficult, but he had seen Reyes at work. He had seen how a single person with a single vision could come within a hair's breadth of pulling it off, even in this weirdly complex system where nothing is real.

Torrance's despair settled into something that might someday resemble fortitude.

Yes, he could still make a difference.

But to do so meant he had to plan.

Take a while to rest, maybe. Let the world run on its own for a bit. Play the game, find the levers, maybe be the father to a kid who would eventually grow up to leave him like Kitchell was, and be the partner of a high-profile military woman while he silently filled the spaces that could let him guide certain decisions.

Yes, he thought. It was time to play the long game.

"Thank you, Thomas," he said. "I can't wait to see you tonight."

NEWS

SOURCE: INFOWAVE — NEWS for the 23rd century
TRANSMITTED: November 11, 2222, Earth Standard
HEADLINE: UG Space Crew Finds Ancient Civilization

United Government Interstellar Command spokesperson Casper Gran confirmed today that the crew of the UGIS Hercules, *the ninth Excelsior class spacecraft to be built, and the first to be used for partial scientific purposes, has discovered relics of a civilization in the Sigma Draconis system. The data sheet, distributed shortly after the broadcast, indicates that rubidium-strontium dating suggests the location is roughly 700 million years old.*

"We're excited at the discovery," Gran said. "Unfortunately we are several hundred million years too late to shake hands."

The site was described as a small village.

Fossil records suggest life-forms existed, including an apelike reptilian animal that met its demise through a volcanic eruption.

The exercise was brought to a halt when Universe Three raiders drove the science crew out of the area.

"It's a shame we're just finding this," Gran said in reply to a question as to whether skirmishes with members of the terrorist faction Universe Three had affected their progress. "It's very hard to do good science when you're facing attacks every time you turn your back. So, yes, it's slowing us down, but I'm sure we'll return."

SOURCE: INFOWAVE — NEWS for the 23rd century
TRANSMITTED: April 19, 2223, Earth Standard
HEADLINE: First Interstellar Colony Settled

UG officials announced the successful landing and installation of the Freehold colonists on Florecer, the innermost planet in the 16 Cygni B system.

The colony represents the first public commercial venture to come from the Star Drive program, and has been sponsored by the United Government Consortium for Advancement of Humanity, a corporate think tank that has recently been making a controversial splash for their advanced concepts on the use of capitalism to drive progress into the stars.

"This is an important day for us," said consortium spokesperson Allegra Hopkins. "It's exciting to know that we have a place where human beings can live and grow out in the stars."

The establishment of the colony also represents Interstellar Command's latest approach at providing security against Universe Three attacks.

"The Command has dedicated an entire wing to the garrison and defense of Florecer," Hopkins said. "For which we are grateful."

In related news, scientists have discovered a striated methane and sulfuric atmosphere over the third planet in the Omicron Eridani system. "We don't think the planet is one we would want to settle. It's not as pleasant as Florecer," joked Io-based Cal State University professor Leif Womar. "But we're certain that we can grow biological material there, and we're interested in determining if we can use it as an interstellar agricultural center."

The United Congresses are apparently considering a joint effort to place a bioengineering station in orbit around the planet in hopes the remote farming techniques could result in Omicron Eridani being converted into a food services facility.

SOURCE: INFOWAVE — NEWS for the 23rd century
TRANSMITTED: October 6, 2229, Earth Standard
HEADLINE: 70 Ophiuchi A: No Life

UG scientists announced they have come up empty again in their search for extraterrestrial life. UGIS Terraplane, *the newest Star Drive spacecraft, completed a two-month mission to the 70 Ophiuchi A system, where six planets and their twelve moons were scanned for signs of life.*

"We are disappointed but not overly surprised," Chief Engineer Samuel Berk explained at a Lester Space Research Center press conference. "It's a very big universe out there, and we're looking for a needle in a haystack. We remain confident, though. Star Drive technology means it won't be too long before we've had a look-see at most of the nearby galaxy."

The UG space program has been facing controversy over the size of its budget, and several opponents have begun calling for a curtailing of planned missions in order to save resources and focus on the Universe Three attacks that are still wreaking havoc in many wild territories.

SOURCE: INFOWAVE — NEWS for the 23rd century
TRANSMITTED: May 7, 2231, Earth Standard
HEADLINE: Search for Terrorists Continue

After a pattern of recent attacks struck stations on Mars, Uranus, and the asteroid mining belt, UG Interstellar Command officials released declassified data describing the methods being used to triangulate the possible whereabouts of Universe Three's central location.

"Given the time we've been involved in these skirmishes, it would not be surprising if the renegades have split into multiple outposts," said Sector Admiral Omir Lassiter. "As such we're deploying listening telescopes and other ground-based processing personnel to keep our feelers out." The analysts are tasked with identifying radio emissions that reach the Solar System, and comparing them to data recorded during the multiple jump operations being taken to study various sectors of space.

Critics suggest that the approach is too lackadaisical.

"The latest round of attacks have proven once again that the current administration does not care about the people of the Solar System and our colonies," said newly announced candidate for supreme president, Tomas Halper.

Halper, who previously ran the Kanisco Agricultural Conglomerate and has spent a decade Earthside working on corporate policy, announced his candidacy amid speculation that his backers include many in the military complex.

Sector Admiral Lassiter does not agree with Halper's assessment.

"Space is very big, of course," Lassiter said. "But our mission planners have devised a fail-safe method of canvasing the nearby starfields. We believe the recent increase in frequency of attacks show that even Universe Three understands that it's now just a matter of time before we find them in our crosshairs."

SOURCE: INFOWAVE — NEWS for the 23rd century
TRANSMITTED: December 21, 2233, Earth Standard
HEADLINE: U3 Cripples Florecer Agricultural Centers

For the first time, Universe Three has attacked the remote colony of Florecer, destroying much of its local agricultural business center, and leaving several of the infrastructural systems the facility needs to sustain itself in shambles.

In a profile that has become horrifyingly routine, field reports note that Universe Three skimmers performed bombing and strafing runs across the establishment's eastern regions for thirty minutes before returning to their ships and jumping out. It left food stores blazing, destroyed the waste processing plant, and shattered the primary dam that helps the colony manage its water.

The attack brought a fresh round of bitter attacks on the terrorist organization, and upon Deidra Francis, their reclusive leader.

"As we always do, our people will band together over this," said Supreme President Halper. "I have already directed the purchase of food stock being developed across the entire structure of our Solar System's vast capabilities. We will not allow Universe Three to distract us from who we are."

SOURCE: INFOWAVE — NEWS for the 23rd century
TRANSMITTED: August 16, 2235, Earth Standard
HEADLINE: Earth Farmers Band against "Alien" Growers

Farmers gathered in an Iowa cornfield, where they stomped a field of nearly ripe corn to the ground to protest the sale of alien crops in Earth markets. For several years growers have fought efforts to allow colonies in the Delta Pavonis, Tau Ceti, and Eta Cassiopeia systems to have access to their markets.

The protest was held on a farm owned by Henri Armbrister, whose family has managed agricultural businesses since 1900.

"I lost a full crop, but it made our point," Armbrister said. "Foreign farmers have given the government millions of solar dollars."

Several farmers explained they were worried about viruses, bacteria, and "other space bugs" being released into the Earth's food supply if corn from off-world colonies were to be imported.

"We have no data to justify that fear," Representative Cash Naru said. "The nutrient content of the soil is different in various systems, so the chemical compositions of foreign corn will vary to an extent. In addition, growth patterns are obviously different because of diverse harvesting seasons across the wide array of environments we have in our network—we get three crops a season from Tau Ceti Warsaw, for example, where we get only two from Iowa. But science has proven that corn grown in the Delta Pavonis system is no less healthy than corn grown in the heartland."

SOURCE: INFOWAVE — NEWS for the 23rd century
TRANSMITTED: June 2, 2244, Luna Communications Center
HEADLINE: Supreme President Halper Elected to Third Term,
Predicts "Decades of Prosperity"

Amid constant news of war on multiple fronts across the galaxy, United Government Supreme President Tomas Halper accepted the election results that provided him a third term.

"The people have spoken," Halper said. "And I am humbled to respond."

The supreme president spoke for forty-five minutes, touching on several campaign issues including tax rates, laws for colonial rights, and the accusations that he has purposefully extended the war with Universe Three and several copycat terrorist organizations in order to keep the population in fear.

"There has never been a better time to be a human being," he said. "We are populating the stars, poverty is a thing of the past, and our ability to create and deliver a high quality of life continues to be on the right path. I expect we'll have decades of prosperity coming as we grow into the uncharted areas of our galaxy."

He did not make any comments regarding the bill he expected the United Congresses to send him that would increase military spending by 72.5 trillion solar dollars, nor did he take questions.

THE MESSAGE

CHAPTER 10

Apogee
Local Date: C198D12
Local Time: 2/9:45

The physics required was a complex array of quantum geometry and multidimensional tensor theory. Dr. Catazara was the man who found the critical path forward, though he passed three years before he could see the final form of the equations, and before the simulations proved it could be done.

As the math evolved, Deidra wanted to understand it.

It didn't help that she had a civilization to support—that the leadership council agreed that spreading the Universe Three presence as far across the 37 Gem system as their numbers would support was important. And it didn't help that the war efforts had to be maintained. It added up to say her days were packed.

Still, she struggled hard, met with Catazara and his team often, had the team send her notes which she studied at night until she fell asleep.

She could conceive the geometries and the use of the exotic matter shunts the team envisioned, but even after years of effort and hundreds of personal interviews with the science team, Deidra now admitted she would never fully comprehend the extra-dimensional math it took to cap the equations.

Her brain just would not twist that way.

So, yes, the physics were hard.

But the final plan, when it all came together, was amazingly simple—far more pedestrian than the math it took to enable, anyway. Multi-dimensional physics would never be simple, but creating a surprise plan generally wasn't that hard—just figure out what the other person expects, and don't do that.

No, Deidra thought as *Icarus* launched and she stood alone on the control station floor, the hard part of this plan didn't lie in its creation.

Nor was it trying to sell the plan to the rest of Universe Three's Leadership. After thirty years of leading raids and organizing development of what was currently five separate outposts on three of the system's planets, Deidra had a handle on how to approach them, and the fact was that news regarding the United Government's efforts to find Universe Three's home had been flowing long enough that everyone knew the UG's random explorations would eventually result in the Solar System's scouts stumbling upon them. The only variable was time.

Some simulations gave Universe Three as few as five standard years, others as many as fifty.

So it hadn't been hard to get the leadership council to okay the plan.

The hard part was when Katriana Martinez looked her in the eye and told her she was volunteering.

Seeing the depth of commitment in the older woman's gaze.

Feeling the passion in her voice as Katriana told her what it meant to her.

"It's too much to ask," Deidra said.

"I want to do it for my girls," Katriana replied as she took Deidra's hands. "I want to be the one who lets us live free."

The hardest part of all was knowing there was only one answer that made sense to give.

"Initial jump complete," the controller's voice came over the intercom.

As she watched telemetry from *Icarus* fade from the mission screen, Deidra felt fractured, but complete.

If it had been anyone other than Katriana, the depth of the lesson here may not have stuck with her—the actual idea that Universe Three absolutely had to find a way to live free, fully untethered from the Uglies, and what that idea really meant may not have fully registered.

As it was, though, the lesson stuck.

Deidra already admired Katriana Martinez beyond doubt, but it was her insistence in running this mission that confirmed for Deidra exactly why Universe Three existed in the first place.

She sighed.

"Are you all right, Director Francis?"

It was Allie Feder, an intern who had been working on the pods that would be used to deliver the final connection, and who Deidre understood was being groomed for a big future. Feder stood beside Deidre, tall and thin, dressed in dark pants and a crisply pressed top made of fiber that had been milled on Apogee. Her face was unlined. Her skin glowed with an amberlike beauty.

The sound of her voice snapped the rest of the control room into place.

Deidre took it in.

The energy of the people here was palpable. The room buzzed with certainty and confidence. The links between these people could not have been more obvious if they were physically tied to each other—the teams each working in their own places, each depending on each other to succeed. No group more important, or less so, than the next.

A weight came off her shoulders.

It as the strangest thing she had ever felt.

Her heart ached beyond her ability to describe. But her soul was singing.

Looking at Allie, it was suddenly not hard to remember that at one time Deidra herself had been that young. She had struggled. She learned how to lead on the job, which meant that she fought her self-doubt in private while publicly keeping on her game face.

It was hard.

Sometimes she wondered what the hell she was doing.

But from this point on, Deidra would never again doubt.

"Yes," she said to Allie Feder. "I think I'm fine."

CHAPTER 11

Mars: Kochi Station
Local Date: June 2, 2252
Local Time: 1200

The process ran, as it did every day.

It started with a Very Large Array spread over the three hundred square kilometers of Martian surface that comprised Kochi Station observatory. Each day Kochi, and several other observatories for that matter, compressed data and transmitted it on tightbeam laser to a receiver in Earth orbit, where it was then split and forwarded to several other destinations—one being a computer in an office on a mountaintop in Chile.

There, a program that had been written by a student many years before stored the data in overlapping fifteen-minute segments and compared these fresh radio emissions to stored files of noise *Everguard* had recorded during its last mission. Depending on the outcome of this comparison, various routines filed records, updated logs, and categorized the data.

A messaging routine forwarded results to a communications server, where—each morning—Thomas Kitchell's personal system picked them up and performed some additional comparisons.

This particular morning, when these last comparisons finished, a new routine toggled on. A loop that had never been executed before was finally executed, and a new file was created, encapsulated in a security shell, then dropped into the holding bin.

At the same time, a notification flag began to pulse in Kitchell's personal account.

CHAPTER 12

Crystal City, Virginia
Local Date: June 3, 2252
Local Time: 0507

For all the time Torrance had spent dealing with such events, you would think he could handle this kind of thing. There had been worse abuses in the past, of course, some of which he had even participated in. But for some reason, the news this morning bothered him.

SOURCE: INFOWAVE — NEWS for the 23rd century
   TRANSMITTED: June 1, 2252, Earth Standard
   HEADLINE: Parkridge, Inc., Renames Planet

. . .

Parkridge Mining Company announced that it will rename the fourth planet in the Tau Ceti system Parkridge Four. The company purchased the planet three Earth weeks ago for an estimated 25 trillion solar dollars.

"This step ensures the integrity of our brand as we move even further into the space age," Maya, the spokesmodel for the company, said in the corporation's video release. The model wore a white pantsuit and the new Parkridge line of cosmetics.

Parkridge Four's atmosphere is nearly 100 percent chlorine, making it inhospitable to human life. The company, however, has engineered their production processes to use that atmosphere itself as a scrubber device to remove toxins while processing their full product suite of industrial-grade solvents. "We will be using the entire planet as a production facility," Maya said in the release. "No part will be wasted."

I'm getting too old for this, Torrance thought as he checked the trim of his sideburns in the bathroom mirror of his room in the Kendra Hotel. Seventy may be the new sixty, but getting older still sucked. This spring marked his thirty-seventh year in the ambassadorial sector—all of them as a science liaison officer, none of them particularly exciting.

He was doing his best to stay in physical shape: An hour in the rec club every day. Skipping dessert. Monitoring his sleep. Every night he ran a bio scan. The numbers were as perfect as could be expected. On the other hand, while extending a man's telomeres may double his life, the signs of age remained as obvious as rings on a tree stump.

Lines and dry patches marred his skin. His crew cut was shorter than he used to wear, but the hair was thinning and graying to white anyway, so it looked better this way. Even his eyes were worn and faded. He pursed his lips. This was not how he expected his career to have gone.

The Kendra was a high-rise overlooking the western shore of the Potomac River.

Willim Pinot—the chief intelligence officer of the United Government Intelligence Office—expected him at 0700 and Torrance still hadn't had breakfast.

He sighed, then ran a brush over his scalp.

The CIO had been vague about the agenda, and politics always left Torrance uneasy, even after thirty-seven years of playing the game.

He stepped back from the mirror and yanked his jacket to the side so that his buttons were aligned and his shoulders square. He was seventy-one locals—no longer the slender "kid" he had been on *Everguard*—but he still presented the uniform with a bit of dignity. If he ever *did* decide to do something rash like retire, he would miss the uniform as much as anything else. He strapped his personal comm system over his forearm, punched up his temperature and blood sugar, and glanced at the time.

That was when he first noticed the red icon flashing.

———

To the few who knew about them—or at least remembered them—the Eden files had been destroyed with *Everguard*. No great loss. Images of storms on desolate planets are interesting only to a handful of scientists and hobbyists. But to Torrance, the *Everguard* files had always been like hand-inked parchment stuffed in green bottles that were floating on the currents of the most massive sea known to humanity. They were words sent from unknown people who lived on Alpha Centauri A's second planet. To hell with folks who said life couldn't exist there—he knew better.

Once, Torrance thought he had made inroads with a professor, but it turned out she had only listened to his arguments because she needed ideas for two of her students' dissertations, who both were working in science journalism rather than in any serious technical field. They interviewed him, and set him up with a modeler, who turned the noise into a set of intriguing posters and a piece of multidimensional art.

Another time he spent a week with Lars Messier, an astrobiologist who, it turned out, had just signed a contract with an entertainment company and wanted to use Torrance's experience for an episode of *Strange and Unexplained*, a series that examined a collection of what were mostly sensationalistic events that no one actually believed were true. Messier waited until the very last hour of the last day, just before recording was to begin, to tell Torrance that their earlier interviews were really just preludes to a show, and to ask him to sign the release forms. "Just a formality, really," Messier said as he put the legal pad in front of Torrance.

He still remembered the smell of spicy mustard in the sandwich line of the buffet the production crew was setting up.

"We just need to make the episode now."

It had been the lowest point of Torrance's efforts.

Other than those two opportunities, a career spent with planetary scientists hadn't resulted in any real progress.

That was why he had kept up with Thomas Kitchell's work as the kid went through every new stage in his career: a stint at LUMI, an assignment in the Interstellar Command's Cosmological Center, three standards spent in comet analysis, where his part in using quantum foam sound analysis to map entire swathes of the space in near real-time won him the prestigious LiKay Award, and a grant that he then spent digging deeper into Alpha Centauri and her planets. As the years passed, Thomas Kitchell had become one of the Solar System's most prestigious minds when it came to deep space signal processing. The kid had done work on a hundred key questions, including spear-heading a group that was focused on sensing possible locations for Universe Three outposts. As far as Torrance knew, it was Thomas Kitchell's efforts that had key Interstellar Command people suggesting that the time scale to discovery was now years rather than decades.

Kitchell's reputation was why Torrance was depressed for days after each time he heard Kitchell had again come up empty.

It was why he had kept studying the files himself for years as he had been stationed at Tau Ceti and Delta Pavonis and all the others, even though it became more and more obvious that Torrance didn't have the skills required to crack the code. Working on the files was important to him. To him, they would always mean something.

They had always been there for him.

They had given him solace.

They gave him a sense of self.

They gave him a place to retreat to when the girls came—Mercedes first, then Eliana—and he proved beyond doubt that he was awkward as a father.

The files were something he could control when everything else was elusive. Even after all these years, he could plug them into his system and listen to the pops and hisses of the music they contained. Of course, that was probably why Marisa finally gave up on him again.

Torrance had never been a very successful family man, even when he was trying, and you can only retreat from problems so many times.

Now he studied them out of habit more than anything else.

They were familiar.

They stayed by his side even after the scientific community had laughed him out of their inner circle. Nothing, it seems, ostracizes a man so fully as thinking outside the accepted.

Still…

Too much of his life was tied up in these files. The fact that the scientific community hadn't accepted the idea of life on Eden couldn't force Torrance to give up.

Now the icon was flashing on his personal comm system.

"Thomas," he answered. "How good to hear from you."

"LC," Kitchell replied.

Even with just those two syllables, the tone of Kitchell's voice was odd. It reminded Torrance of the time when Kitchell was a teenager. He half expected the word *edge* to come out soon.

"I need you to check your secure data server," Kitchell said.

"Tell me more."

"No time now. But I need you to look at something."

———

Bypassing breakfast, Torrance accessed his home unit. The screen changed to a familiar interface panel. He pulled reports and examined Kochi extracts. Automatic sorting routines charted key graphs. The passage of time faded to a blur. An hour later Torrance sat on the edge of his bed, deliriously dizzy.

A new signal had been received.

It would have been just a ball of noise to most observers, but Kitchell had pulled it apart and placed it against the data from Eden.

The correlation was solid—full-spectrum frequency matches in nearly every frame. They had no idea of what the signal said or meant, but the two had matches at almost every frequency. Same power densities. Same peak-to-peak gaps. These signals made a strong case for the idea that they came from the same source.

This was no storm.

This was a created wave.

A message transmitted by a machine.

A machine built by someone capable of building machines.

The world was suddenly small but expansive, understood but unfathomable.

It would take weeks of hard work to make the data presentable to anyone else, but Torrance understood the massive truth embedded here like it was a block of granite sitting on his chest.

Life existed outside the Solar System.

The kid had done it. Thomas Kitchell had proven the fact of some form of intelligence on Eden.

His heart burst. He wanted to cry, wanted to hug someone, wanted to run into the streets and shake people by the shoulders or kiss them on the cheeks or just hold them tightly and howl at the sky like the crazy old men in the Arazorn colony.

He wanted…well. Mostly he just wanted to tell someone.

But the room was empty and quiet.

The heating system kicked on.

The bed sat unmade, sheets wadded and rumpled at the foot.

He rubbed his eyes and closed his system. His lips were dry and parched. He glanced at his watch. Forty-five minutes to get to Pinot's office.

He picked up his hat from the dresser and checked the mirror. Crisp. He smiled and gave himself a salute. He looked crisp.

Politics be damned, there wasn't a thing in the world Willim Pinot could tell him today that would get him down.

CHAPTER 13

Arlington, Virginia
Local Date: June 3, 2252
Local Time: 0700

Torrance took the underground walkway to the monorail transfer and got off at Arlington. The bioscanner allowed him to take the purple line from there. This was Wilson Cross—a shelter dug deep under the eastern foothills of the Appalachian Mountains, a place where every door warranted a security code and every wall was made of reinforced concrete that had been lined with radiation-hardened composites. His lighthearted mood gave the process of navigating checkpoints a feeling more like playing secret agent than its usual baggage of paranoid scrutiny.

Everything seemed so real—the smell of his escort's boot polish, the echoes of footsteps in the underground hallway, the dryness of cool air, the escort's name spelled in clean white letters on a black badge. The corridors were tight and brightly lit, the walls painted standard-issue beige. Image projectors at regular intervals gave the area a professional flare. Even the metallic clangs of tri-level stainless steel security doors could not dampen his spirits.

They came to a doorway. A crimson laser flashed his optic nerve. The door slid open.

"Good morning, sir," Torrance said as he stepped forward.

"Good morning, Ambassador," Pinot answered in a graveled voice, motioning to a padded blue chair without looking up from his desktop screen. "Have a seat."

Willim Pinot had grown up inside the intelligence office, and was arguably the most powerful man in the Solar System. He sat in his chair, but Torrance could still tell he had a gawky height to him that made him more imposing. Black eyes sat like a pair of polished marbles above rounded cheekbones, and his nose was upturned and flattened. A scraggly, gray-laced goatee grew in a sprawl around his lips. His shirt was white and open one button at the collar. It was early, yet already rings of sweat darkened the area under his armpits.

Torrance sat while Pinot marked something on his screen.

Pinot's dress coat hung from a rack in the far corner. Paperwork cluttered his desktop. The leather chair squealed as the CIO put his stylus down, sat forward, and clasped his hands together.

"Can Tailor get you coffee?"

"That would be good, thank you."

Pinot spoke to the computer. "Coffee, please. Sugar." He paused and looked at Torrance. "Cream?"

Torrance shook his head.

"No cream."

Pinot smiled.

"I suppose you wonder why you are here."

"The question has crossed my mind."

"I need you to kill a man."

"Sir?"

"You heard me."

"But…" Torrance squirmed in his chair. "I'm not an assassin."

"Correct." Pinot nodded matter-of-factly. "You are a scientist—an engineer, actually, but close enough for government work, right?"

Torrance frowned.

"I am in the unique spot, you see, of needing someone who is both a scientist *and* an assassin. Since I have no time to train an assassin to be a scientist, I think it wiser to go the opposite direction. Don't you agree?"

"I…guess so," Torrance heard himself say.

The door opened and Pinot's aide entered with a coffee service.

An edgy Colombian aroma filled the room. The sound of liquid flowing over china was ritualistic in the silence. Pinot motioned the aide to ignore his coffee cup in lieu of the double-sized mug on his desk.

The aide left.

Torrance lifted a cup and cradled it in his palm. The coffee warmed the thin cup quickly. He sipped, blowing briefly to avoid scalding. He wished he had eaten something now.

"The Galactic Council on Wormhole Physics is being held next week," Pinot said simply. "You will attend, and you will kill Emil Pentabill."

"Oscar?"

"Yes, that is, I suppose, what his friends call him."

"I can't kill anyone, better yet a friend."

"Yet, that is your job."

"If I refuse?"

Pinot gulped his coffee, then set his mug amid loose paper on his desk. "I'm certain neither of your ex-wives will care one way or the other. God knows I can vouch for the disinterest of ex-wives. And I know you're not really close to your daughters, but surely they need their old man around, don't you think?"

Torrance squeezed his lips into a tight line. He loved Ana and Mercy. But something had always gotten in the way while they were growing up—a conference to attend, or a seminar to facilitate.

There was a war on, after all.

Despite the expansion they had been able to achieve, there was always a war on, anymore. People were always dying in faraway places, sometimes as fast as they could be shipped out.

He had never had enough time.

He had lost Marisa just as he had lost Adrienne before her. And he was gone while his daughters went from crawling to kindergarten to high school to college to careers of their own.

Pinot's threat, however, was clear and direct. Kill or be killed.

"Why Pentabill?"

"The man is a confirmed traitor."

"I've known Oscar for years," Torrance said. "I find that very hard to believe."

"Yet still true."

Torrance shook his head.

"You want evidence?" Pinot pointed to a brown data cube on the corner of his desk.

Torrance picked it up. The cube was small, its edges sharp and prickly.

"Read it at your leisure."

"What's on it?"

"Proof that Universe Three got to him years ago—before, even, your cruise with *Everguard*. Standard espionage stuff. Find a source, start early and small until they're hooked, then raise the ante. By the end, Pentabill sold them the Star Drive, and several techniques for manufacturing exotic matter—specifically including solutions to throat tensors, I might add—and, of course, Kransky-Watt."

Torrance grimaced outwardly.

Kransky and Watt were the first to demonstrate that the kinetic flow of a star's energy could be fed back into a wormhole's gate fields, thereby providing traversable stability. The throat tensors were needed to understand and build the most critical juncture in the wormhole system. It was this technology that had allowed the engineers to draw energy from the interior of Alpha Centauri A to power Star Drive engines, and hence open up the galaxy to faster-than-light travel.

Without the information Pentabill had sold, Universe Three could not have developed their own wormholes. Without those wormholes, they could not have sustained a galaxy-faring fleet. And without a galaxy-faring fleet, they could not have waged the war that had killed so many young men and women over the past four standard decades.

"Oscar is a very bright man," Torrance said.

"All the more reason to make an example of him."

"You want me because you think I can attend the council without arousing suspicion in advance of the strike."

"A good assassin blends in."

"You're overestimating my status considerably."

Pinot gave a sarcastic huff. "You don't have to explain to me that you are no longer one of the scientific elite, Captain. I know this." He raised a pointed index finger. "But this is an advantage for you with regard to this mission. Your compatriots will accept your attendance, but will keep you at arm's length. It will be quite easy for you to fade into the woodwork at an appropriate time."

Pinot's straightforward dissection of Torrance's standing stung.

"So I'm a Trojan horse?" Torrance said. "A wolf in sheep's clothing?"

"Trojan horse," Pinot said as he rubbed his goatee. A smile creased his cheeks with a series of abstract folds that made him look like a washed-out coconut. "I like that."

The concept of killing in cold blood was suddenly very real.

Torrance drank coffee and put the cup back on the tray. The liquid ate the lining of his stomach and did nothing to help his dry throat.

"I can't do it," he said. The pleading quality in his voice made him feel weak and somehow ashamed.

"Men are always capable of more than they think."

"It's not like that," Torrance lied too quickly. He thought about the signal he had received this morning. "I'm *not* afraid of it. It's just...I have a new project I need to look into."

"Really? I reviewed your assignments with Ambassador Cash yesterday. She made no mention of new projects."

"It's..." Torrance looked at Pinot. The CIO was enjoying himself. He was playing a game, a fisherman who had set his hook and was now letting Torrance run but keeping the line taut.

"She doesn't know about it," Torrance finally said.

"Then it can't be too important, now, can it?"

"Only discovery of a new life-form."

Pinot sat back in his chair. "We're not going through this again, are we?"

Talking about the signals here felt wrong, but he couldn't help himself.

"We've confirmed cohesive signals from Eden. No mistaking it."

"Don't trifle with me, Captain. Universe Three is nearly done, now. They aren't rich enough to support spacecraft development at the rate we can, and they've stretched themselves so thin that they are now scattered into little pockets of resistance with little chance of succeeding. After fifty years of bloodshed, we are winning. Very close to wiping the galaxy clean of them—too close to the ultimate victory to allow me any leeway in letting you shirk this final duty."

"We've only been at war with U3 for thirty-seven years," Torrance said, feeling spiteful joy at being able to correct the administrator.

Pinot's smile was gruesome as it was sadistic.

"What?"

"You don't think this war started with the Cassiopeia incident, do you?" Pinot chuckled and sat back with his intertwined fingers lying over his belly. "Let me ask you a question. Were you aware that *Everguard* sailed without a ship's intelligence officer?"

Torrance thought of Government Security Officer Casey. A government security officer was not an intelligence officer, and vice versa, and he knew that Casey did not originate from Pinot's office.

"Yes."

"Didn't that strike you as odd?"

"I never thought about it. I figured Admiral Hatch or Captain Romanov forced him out or something else political must have happened. I didn't think it was a big issue, though. After all, we still had a government security officer. How many enemies would we expect to find in the Alpha Centauri system?"

"Obviously more than you would think."

Torrance gave a dry swallow, but he wasn't lying when he said he had never considered the situation on *Everguard* before.

"Do you really expect this office would allow a ship as important as *Everguard* to sail without an SIO merely because a simpleton admiral thought he could do a better job of it?"

Torrance thought back, his memory fogged by time. Pinot was right about the strength of the intelligence office—even back then. If they wanted an SIO aboard, it's almost certain they could have had one.

"So the intelligence organization left their guy off on purpose?"

"That's true."

"But if you suspected the ship would be the target of an attack…" An idea struck him so cold his fingers felt charged with electricity. He felt his face blanch.

Pinot cocked his head and arched an eyebrow.

Christ. It couldn't be. Could it?

"You are catching on, aren't you?"

"You knew *Everguard* was going to be attacked."

"Of course we did. Or, at least we knew it was likely."

Torrance pressed his fingers hard into the armrests of the chair. "Why didn't you stop it?"

"The intelligence office has been at war with Universe Three since the day of U3's inception, Captain. It is our job to control these groups. But the sorry truth of the matter is that our system makes it very difficult to be as aggressive as we need to be without an obvious political reason."

"So you stood by and watched as Universe Three destroyed *Everguard*?"

"It is an unfortunate truth that sometimes people have to be sacrificed to the greater good."

"Sacrificed?" The word felt sharp.

"As an ambassador, you understand this better than most."

"If *Everguard* hadn't been attacked, U3 wouldn't have been flushed," he said, beginning to understand fully.

"When a cancer is in your body, it is best cut out before it grows malignant."

"But it backfired, didn't it? The government was going to give U3 their independence…until *Orion's* mission failed."

Pinot laughed. "I wouldn't say *Orion* failed, Torrance—at least not completely. Thanks to you, anyway."

Torrance stared at Pinot. "Douglas and Yuan were the fall guys."

The CIO smiled. "Not everyone who works in our organization wears our stripes, Captain, but many do."

"Jesus," Torrance said, swallowing hard again against anxiety. "Anyone else?"

"The intelligence office is full of invisible heroes."

"Why are you telling me this?"

"You need to understand that this mission I've assigned you is merely one small piece in a very large puzzle, Captain. I want you to see how much has been on the line. And I want you to understand that I will not stand idly by and see any part of the operation fail and imperil the final success of the entire effort."

Torrance clenched his jaw.

The words *you can't make me* nearly came off his tongue. But that was wrong. Willim Pinot's entire career was about making people do things they wouldn't normally do.

Their meeting was done.

The parameters of his choice lay before him.

Torrance looked across the table and saw confidence and certainty unyielding like an undertow.

Kill or be killed.

As he prepared for bed later that night, Torrance tried to convince himself that his decision to take the assignment hinged on the belief that he had more to do in life, that it was the only way to save Eden. But Torrance had never been very good at shielding himself from what he truly thought.

In the end it all boiled down to the simple fact that he was afraid to die.

CHAPTER 14

Florecer: Galactic Council on Wormhole Physics
Local Date: Third Quarter, Setting 13
Local Time: 1612

A week after meeting with the CIO, Torrance found himself on Florecer, the innermost planet of the 16 Cygni B system, a tiny type-K star some twelve light-years from the Solar System. He sat in the convention center conference auditorium, glancing nervously across the way at Oscar Pentabill. The chairs were large and cushioned, arranged in elevated circles around a central podium. The configuration made the conference feel more like a political debate than a scientific gathering—a fact that brought him a sardonic smile as he sipped chilled water and listened to scientists from around the galaxy argue.

"Alpha Centauri A is going to run out of energy, and we've got to find a way to keep the spacecraft attached to it flying."

"It was supposed to last ten thousand years."

"That assumed the star fueled only a single spacecraft."

"So we're supposed to trust the government this time, too?"

"Don't be an extremist, Vlad. The original estimate also assumed seventy percent flow conversion. Reality is closer to twenty-five."

"That's because Kransky-Watt is so horribly wasteful."

"Reality is their fault?"

"Would you suggest the missions not be flown, and the war lost?"

"There's the problem, then, isn't it?"

Heads nodded.

Torrance sat quietly, watching. Nothing positive was coming from this discussion, and, maybe ironically, he felt a bittersweet tingle of, well, let's call it superiority. It wasn't that he felt good. He didn't want to feel good right now. His assignment was cowardly and vile. The idea of killing Pentabill sat in his gut like cold oatmeal. It would change him forever. But he felt something important as he watched these people bickering. This was only a stage, he realized, a place where names came to rub elbows with other names. Hermann, Yang, Jacob—pick a name, they were here.

No truth was being discovered at this conference.

No science was being performed.

Science was done in labs and behind consoles.

Science, at its core, was an endeavor one undertook in isolated groups, developing results to bring back to the entire community for review. It was the way of the world—the way of history. Bring ideas and you create spaghetti. Bring hard data and you change the world.

Now Torrance had data.

Late at night, between the seemingly never-ending briefings and training programs that UGIO agents had been stuffing into his head, he had been working with Thomas Kitchell to review Kitchell's work and package the information about the most recent Alpha Centauri emissions into a presentable paper. The effort left him tired and drained. His stamina dropped off earlier in the evenings than it once did, and he had not progressed as far as he wanted. But it was good work, and he was proud of it.

If they played it right, it would make Kitchell into a superstar, and Torrance into…well, it would add to whatever he already was in ways he wasn't sure how to predict. But in the end, that didn't matter to

Torrance any more. Not really. What mattered to him, he discovered, was only that he might be able to actually help the defenseless creatures who were now stuck in their home planet, a planet that was almost certainly being bled to death as their sun was stolen from them.

Most current estimates said that Alpha Centauri A would remain viable for something short of four hundred years. Only a few short generations, really. Assuming they could handle the distress to their homeland that was clearly going to happen, and was almost certainly already happening.

Thinking about it was enough to make him sick, but at least he was doing something about it now.

Watching this debate go on around him, he was no longer certain he could say that about this collection of people he once admired, and even perhaps had once thought of as friends.

"No." A wavering voice came amplified through the PA. "That is not the problem at all."

The room shuffled nervously as Fredric Parson stood on rickety knees, gripping a brown cane. His back was bent like a hook. His pate was bald and mottled.

Dr. Parson was 148 years old and living on his last telomere extension. Torrance flashed on their earlier squabble all those years ago. Parson was crotchety even back then.

"We are missing the forest for the trees, my friends. The problem has little to do with spacecraft or missions or even the war as a whole. The problem here is that as we drain away the star's fusing material, we leave the trash behind. It's only a matter of time before energy released by the star's fusion engine will be unable to resist the star's gravity. When that happens, Alpha Centauri A will collapse under its own weight."

"Then we get a supernova," Kalista McKenna interjected.

Scientists across the room rolled their eyes to the ceiling as McKenna stood up. The young woman from Colorado University was brilliant, but she didn't know when it was best to be quiet. The membership had given her leeway for two years, but their patience was drawing to an end. Now McKenna stood like a corporate martyr in her white business dress with a scarf of pink and purple showing tastefully from her collar.

"That's a fanciful notion, Kalista," Parson replied. "Centauri A, however, is similar to our own sun. It will not go supernova."

"A star reacts differently when its mass is in flux."

"All theoretical."

"As is everything we do in this field—all we have is theoretical science backed up by computer simulations. I have a new solution that indicates pressure waves caused by transient masses act as a pseudo mass. At the rate we're tapping Alpha Centauri A, its effective mass will rise dramatically. Alpha Cen *will* go supernova, and it will go supernova sooner than most of our models are predicting the star to run out of fuel. The only question that remains unsolved is whether we'll get a black hole or a neutron star in its place."

The sound of clearing throats reverberated.

Chairs rocked backwards.

Torrance nearly snickered aloud at the level of discomfort around the room. Admittedly, McKenna's idea was brash and most likely wrong. But it was also new and unexpected. Torrance could not help but delight in the ripples the mere suggestion caused this gathering of scientific minds. For the first time, he was actually glad he had come to the council.

Parson's reed-thin voice echoed throughout the center. "All we can really say is that never before have we had an opportunity to learn about this type of an event. We need to prepare. We need to push for new programs and more funding."

"Hear, hear."

A smattering of low-voiced conversations ensued.

Torrance thought they were preparing to move to the next item on the agenda, which was to be a review of the less-than-glorious results of the Newton project—an ill-fated effort that several physicists had undertaken to study a concept that would allow remote wormhole creation anywhere in the universe, and potentially render spacecraft, even the vaunted Star Drives, obsolete.

"What if our fanciful friend is correct?" Benaj Ritta from Mars

Colony Kasbian said. "A supernova so close to the Solar System would be a catastrophe."

"Blast it, man! There will be no supernova!"

Torrance sat back to wait out the next cycle of the argument. Academics were so predictable.

He glanced across the chamber.

Emil "Oscar" Pentabill sat quietly in a suit that matched the wiry gray of his hair, listening but not adding to the conversation. He sipped from a white mug, jotted a note or two into his comm system, and glanced around the room, pausing only momentarily to stare at the conversation.

Why had Pentabill done what he had done? Torrance asked himself. What would motivate a man of science to turn his back on the people he worked for? What could take him over the edge of destroying everything he had worked for with a single decision?

The questions angered him.

The whole thing was Pentabill's fault, after all. It was Oscar Pentabill's activity that had resulted in Torrance's assignment.

But Pentabill was not answering Torrance's questions.

Instead, he just sat placidly, and took notes until he got tired of it all, stood up, and hobbled out of the conference center.

Torrance waited a cautious moment, then got up and followed.

CHAPTER 15

Florecer: Galactic Council on Wormhole Physics
Local Date: Third Quarter, Setting 13
Local Time: 1815

The hotel hallway stretched ahead like a launch tunnel. The carpet was green and black with checkered patterns. Torrance looked for room 1512. Downstairs, the reception was beginning—cocktails and hors d'oeuvres at six, dinner at seven, and an informal presentation on FTL aging patterns at nine.

Pinot's agents had given Torrance more details about Oscar Pentabill than he felt comfortable knowing. Pentabill had been married for twenty-three years but had no children. He was a quiet man who avoided the limelight. His habit at such gatherings as this was to eschew social drinks for quiet time in his room with a martini and a trade magazine. He would arrive for dinner a fashionable five minutes late, eat a vegetarian plate, and play with dessert. Then he would excuse himself to turn in.

The number 1512 stood out in relief against the door.

Torrance pulled a magnetic locksmith from his jacket and held it between his index finger and thumb.

The glass vial in his pocket was solid against his thigh. Bionites swam in the clear liquid, ugly critters—creepy crawly things half organic, half machine designed to systematically attack a person's nervous system then dissociate into the cellular realms of his biology.

Torrance's palms were clammy.

The scent of fear mixed with the dry odor of the door's latex paint.

The locksmith clicked against the wall.

The processor spun numbers.

Flickering digits fell into place.

Torrance turned the knob.

The room was beige and yellow—bathroom to the left, bedroom large and comfortable. A netvision rumbled from the far wall. Sheer inner drapes fluttered in the breeze of the open sliding door. The city splayed over the horizon below, a dirty tapestry of gray and blue as Cygni set on the opposite side of the hotel.

Pentabill sat facing the city, his legs propped against the balcony rail. The drapes obscured his shoulders and head. An iced drink sat on a knee-height table—a martini, complete with a local *dashtar* fruit skewered on a green swizzle. A portable reader lay propped on his lap.

The door shut with an audible click.

Pentabill peered around the drapes, his expression more confusion than fear. A nested mat of his hair caught in the breeze.

"Torrance," he said jovially, collecting his drink and standing.

Pentabill must have seen something on Torrance's expression because he froze, one hand on the doorway's frame, the other dropping the reader mechanically to his side. His shoulders slumped. He was tall and slim, probably an athlete when he was a kid.

He swayed as if the drink was not his first.

Torrance put his hand in his pocket. The vial was cold and smooth, its cap small and ridged. The automatic hypo would react to sudden pressure. The injection would be quick and nearly painless.

"I'm sorry it's you, Torrance."

Pinot's evidence left no doubt that Pentabill was guilty. He had to know it was only a matter of time before the United Government would strike back.

"Why did you do it, Oscar?"

Pentabill's hand shook as he drank. "It's worse than you think."

"What do you mean?"

"Universe Three."

"What about them?"

Pentabill tossed the reader onto the bed.

Torrance gave him time.

"Do you ever notice how we talk about decisions in the name of organizations—but organizations never make decisions."

"I understand that."

"I thought Casmir Francis would lead us in the right direction, but he didn't, and his daughter is no better than the rest."

"What are you talking about, Oscar?"

Pentabill waved his drink around. "Doesn't matter, I suppose. Dead men tell no tales, eh?" He chuckled to himself and glanced at Torrance with an impish grin. "I did it, Torrance. Everything. Kransky-Watt. Exotic material."

"Tell me something I don't already know."

"I sold them Newton."

Anxiety was a moth under Torrance's breastbone. Pinot's cube said nothing about Newton. "Why would they want a failed program?"

Pentabill pointed a bony finger. "UG would be best served to not underestimate Universe Three. Bright folks there—some of the best. Catazara went to their side, you know? He did us one better, too. Figured out how to set a remote link. It's trial and error, but within a range of error U3 can create and destroy wormholes anywhere they want."

"You're kidding me," Torrance said.

Pentabill's response was a wry curl of his lip and a shake of his head.

That's why they wanted Newton, Torrance realized.

Newton gave them something that made remote links work.

This meant Universe Three was ahead of the game. The Star Drive gave human beings the ability to travel faster than light, but that was limited to "just" a spaceship. A truly configurable wormhole, though, a door that could be used in "set and forget" mode, would provide the ability to instantaneously step from, say, wherever it was that U3 had their home base, directly to, for example, Earth. And nothing could keep them from bringing along an army of an additional ten thousand people.

"Are you sure?"

"I've seen the work," Pentabill said. He took a slug from his drink. His face was shadowed and drawn. He looked tired. Pentabill's knuckles became white around his glass. "It took a few tries, but Catazara's team has planted the end of a wormhole in the middle of a black hole."

"Holy Mother of God."

"The other end is going into Alpha Centauri A."

Torrance was taken totally aback. "I don't understand."

"Simple math, Torrance. Alpha Centauri A fuels the spacecraft. Kill the star, kill the spacecraft."

"It could be worse than that," Torrance said. "The physics gets calculated as if the black hole were actually inside the star, and we have no way of knowing the mass of the black hole Universe Three is connecting to. A supermassive black hole so close to the Solar System could be dangerous someday."

"Like I said—no better than the rest." Pentabill breathed deeply through his nose, and killed the rest of his drink. "The world protects its own, though, Torrance. I used to believe U3 truly wanted the holistic world they talk about. But the Francises of the world are just card sharps. They speak a great game, but…who knows what's next?"

Torrance shrugged.

"But one thing *I* do believe with all my being," Pentabill continued, "is that Casmir Francis deserved whatever happened to him, and Deidra will deserve no better."

The handle to the door jiggled. Pentabill's face went pale.

"Who is it?" Torrance asked him.

Pentabill looked at Torrance with a pallbearer's grimace.

"Do me a favor?" Pentabill said. "If you get a chance, tell Glory I love her."

The door swung open. A man wearing waiters white blew past Torrance and collided with Pentabill. Pentabill grunted. His glass smashed against the wall with the smell of gin. The man was big and quick—probably juiced. He lifted Pentabill in stride and rushed to the balcony.

Pentabill disappeared over the edge.

He did not scream. Did not even speak.

Torrance anticipated the thick sound of a body hitting the ground, but the impact was not audible.

"You're with Universe Three?" Torrance asked, the truth dawning.

The waiter looked up. He was maybe twenty, with brown hair and an angular face. He flexed his hands, bent, and reached to his pants leg where Torrance could see the bulging shape of a weapon.

Torrance would get only one chance.

He kicked.

The waiter pivoted away and Torrance's foot crashed against the bed railing. His momentum carried him, though, and his body twisted, losing balance, bouncing off the mattress and sprawling to the floor with a lung-crushing thud.

The waiter spun and locked onto him, pressing his weapon to Torrance's temple. The gun was small—a laser system with charge enough for two or three good shots.

Torrance raised one hand.

Kalista McKenna, he thought. Supernova. It was the only idea he had.

"If you kill me, U3 will be making a big, big mistake."

"Tell it to the bosses."

"Let me."

"What?"

"Take me to your bosses, and let me tell them about the mistake."

The waiter put his gun against Torrance's forehead.

"My name is Torrance Black. I'm a scientist from the United Government. U3 is working without critical information. If you do what the man you just tossed off the edge of the world said you're going to do, U3 is liable to blow away most of the civilized galaxy."

The agent's face was impassive.

The weapon's muzzle was cold against Torrance's skull. He hoped his bluff was convincing.

The man's face softened. "I don't want to leave you splattered here anyway."

Torrance nodded. He knew a bit of how this game was played. Soon the nets would carry headlines about Oscar Pentabill's suicide. Another body in the room would ruin that story line.

"Get up and let's go."

Torrance complied, straightening his pants and jacket as he went through the doorway.

The hallway was as quiet as it had been earlier.

Their footsteps were heavy against the carpet, Torrance walking first, the waiter behind with the barrel of the gun pressing against the small of Torrance's back. The fabric of his pants rasped with each stride.

They came to the elevator.

"Get in slow," the waiter said. "Don't want any collateral damage, understand?"

Torrance nodded. "You're as clear as vacuum."

The doors opened. Four people stood in the compartment. The doors were burnished bronze, reflecting images as blobs of color. The air smelled of humid carpet and light cleanser. The waiter edged behind him, the blunt point of the weapon like a fist against his kidney. They stopped on the tenth floor and took on another passenger, then two more on the third-floor mezzanine.

Sweat pooled on Torrance's brow.

What should he do when the doors opened? Run? Turn and punch?

How many people could die with a random laser shot?

The doors opened.

"Left," the man said quietly.

The lobby was large and open, but still crowded.

"Outside."

They walked across the pavilion. An automatic door opened as they approached the exit. The air at ground level was hot and stagnant. A gravcar pulled up and the back door opened to reveal a man in a business suit. Torrance could not see his face, but his hand showed another laser.

"Get in," the waiter said.

Torrance didn't hesitate.

The door slammed. The man was slim and smelled of soap. His hair was long and tied tightly behind his head. He reached across the bench seating.

A pinprick burned on the back of Torrance's hand.

His world went dark.

CHAPTER 16

Somewhere in the deep swirl of dreams, Torrance decided that the question is not whether or not God plays dice. The question is what game he plays.

STARBOUND

CHAPTER 17

U3 Ship *Icarus*
Local Date: Unknown
Local Time: Unknown

"Welcome to *Icarus*, Captain Black." The voice was distant and vaguely feminine.

"Wha—"

Bright light stabbed his temples.

His eyes burned.

A row of fluorescent lights lined the ceiling, ringed with halos of silver and blue. A pallet was hard against his back. Shadows with human form glided through his vision, shifting light like a kaleidoscope.

Torrance was hungry.

Icarus? Why was that name familiar?

The man. A laser. A car. Oscar Pentabill falling.

He took a full breath. Oxygen refreshed his body. Memory

returned. Blinking brought things into better focus. A man in a blue medical uniform stood against the wall. A woman with auburn hair sat in a chair beside the bed.

"Get yourself cleaned up," the woman said, standing. "I'll order you something to eat."

The man leaned forward to read numbers from the monitor over Torrance's head. A guard came into focus on the opposite side of the room. The woman turned to the man in blue. "I'll report he's awake. Get him a shower and some food. Make sure he is presentable."

"Aye, ma'am," he replied.

Sometime later, water rushed over him.

The smell of soap was something normal to hold on to.

The warm sting against his chest and shoulders made him feel human. He was stiff and sore, and the water brought him simple comfort as the world came back to his brain.

Icarus was a carbon copy of *Orion*, both among the first Star Drive spacecraft ever designed, each built in cookie-cutter fashion to save cost and development time. They had been made with maintenance in mind—with service nodes placed at key junctures on every level. Each node provided access to the systems command center through sleek, holographic interfaces, the first to utilize such controls.

Torrance grimaced with the memory of a time when such trivia seemed to matter.

If it was true that Alpha Centauri A was going to be tied to a black hole, he was sitting on a ghost ship.

He wrapped a towel around his waist and stepped into his quarters. His clothes were gone, replaced by a pile on the foot of the bed. The pants were baggy and gray, tied in front with a drawstring. The shirt was blue polyfiber that hung below his hips.

Breakfast was tasteless cornbread and freeze-dried apricots in the officers' mess. A carafe of coffee sat in the middle of the table. An armed guard stood outside.

Simple as it was, the food did wonders for the clarity of his mind.

"Good morning."

Torrance sat up straighter.

The woman who entered the room was middle-aged—maybe sixty, maybe seventy, who could tell. Her yellow blond hair and a dark complexion spoke of Latin heritage. She wore black trousers and a zippered sweatshirt with the *Icarus* logo sewn into the left breast. She was thin to the point of frailty. Her eyes were watery blue with dark half-moons beneath. Her lips turned down at the corners. On the whole, she reminded him of a bird.

He took a swig of coffee and wiped nonexistent crumbs from the corner of his mouth.

The woman took a seat across from him. "I understand you have something you want to tell us?"

"I haven't decided whether to tell you or not."

"Choose your game carefully, Captain. Personally, I don't believe you have a damned thing that could be useful, and I resent the acrobatics we went through to rendezvous with you. But some people think you know something. They think you might actually be able to prove we're making a mistake. Unlike the United Government, U3 actually cares about the galaxy."

"Sure you do. You care just enough to put a black hole right in the Solar System's neighborhood."

"The Solar System is *not* the galaxy. Besides, the people of the Solar System will have quite a bit of time to find someplace else to go if they need to."

"But what if they like where they live?" Torrance said, his thoughts snapping to life-forms on Eden.

"Then they can stay until the end."

Torrance stared with disbelief at the woman. "Who are you?"

"I am Katriana Martinez, captain on *Icarus*. More relevant at this point, I am responsible for forming the black hole link."

"I see."

"And you are Torrance Black, science ambassador, ex-captain in the United Government Interstellar Command, and, on the sly, one of the chief engineers on the Newton project."

Torrance frowned, but gathered himself. He hadn't touched Newton, but he wasn't going to tell Martinez anything now. He supposed it was a good thing that U3's data wasn't airtight.

"Your information is interesting," he said.

"You have two ex-wives and a pair of daughters: Mercedes, who is currently stationed in a cryo research lab on Europa, and Eliana, who graduates this spring from Canal University with a degree in accelerated-growth bioprosthesis. Your first marriage failed at least in part due to certain—" She paused and raised her eyebrow indelicately. "—deficiencies. Because of these same deficiencies both daughters are adopted. They both tell you they live alone. Eliana is actually holed up with another young woman who is studying multidimensional mathematics. Mercedes is preparing to get married, and has been living off and on with the man of her choice for some time."

A chain reaction of images clouded Torrance's mind. Mercy was getting married, and Ana—who had always had such a painful shyness about her—had someone special in her life. Why hadn't they told him? He never thought he was overbearing about such things.

Martinez's stare was filled with accusatory sternness.

She reached into a sweatshirt pocket and set a small vial on the table before her—the bottle Torrance had taken to Oscar Pentabill's room. Cold light from the ceiling reflected from its surface. Martinez put it on its side. It made a hollow sound as she rolled it from hand to hand.

"Do you know what's in here?"

Torrance shrugged, trying not to concentrate on the shiny bottle of microsized death.

"They're bionites, Captain Black."

"Really?" Torrance said with innocence.

Martinez was having none of it.

"Are you threatening me?" Torrance said.

"Why would I need to threaten you? You're already a dead man."

Torrance stared quizzically at her.

"You've surmised that *Icarus* will be destroyed when the black hole is set."

"Yes."

"What you don't know is that *Icarus* has been given the honor of actually creating the link itself. We are nearing launch now."

"We're in the Centauri system?"

"Yes."

"I thought you could set links remotely."

"We can."

"Then why send *Icarus*?"

Martinez smiled. "I'm the one asking questions. You gave us a cryptic warning about blowing up half the galaxy. I want to know what you've got."

Torrance recalled Oscar Pentabill as he said U3 could set links in any location they wanted to *within a range of error.* "You can't control the mechanism yet," Torrance replied. "Your remote capability is fine when you have enough space and time to cast about. But now that you've got a black hole attached to one end, you can't afford to drop the other end willy-nilly, can you?"

The intensity of Martinez's gaze let him know he was right. "Doesn't matter either way, does it?"

"So you'll set a link like *Everguard* did."

"Almost."

"What do you mean, almost?"

Martinez's entire face lit up in a maniacal smile. "*Icarus* herself will be part of the final mission."

"I'm not sure I—" Sudden understanding made his skin contract. He sat, staring dumbly at the ship's first officer. "You're going to set the pods by flying *Icarus* into the star."

"We'll launch some of them directly," she replied. "But as I understand the math and the structure of the star itself, the geometry of the launch requires we keep some behind. Which is fine. It fits our sense of poetry."

Torrance stared at the glass vial Martinez was still rolling on the table. Who was this woman? What had her life been that she was willing to give it away so freely?

"*Icarus* isn't designed to withstand the heat of a star's core like the pods are," Martinez said. "We'll burn up before reaching the proper trigger point, but the ship will get sucked into the wormhole as soon as the pods are activated anyway. So we'll get as close as we can before we launch."

"Well," Torrance said with what he thought was a tone of humor, "that should reduce your probability of error."

Martinez grew smug. "You can see why this might be a good time to talk to me. And why it would be good to be convincing. If you are bluffing, you will die with us, and disappear into so many particles blowing on Centauri's solar wind."

She held the vial still with the fingertips of one hand.

"And if I'm not bluffing?"

Martinez's eyes got bigger. "You tell me."

"We're wasting our time, you know?" Torrance finally said.

"That's what I told Director Francis."

Torrance laughed like he had never laughed before. It was a short laugh, a mere chuckle. But that single noise was filled with the full depth of everything he had learned in this, what he assumed would be, the final moments of his life.

"That's not what I meant."

"Then what exactly is it that you mean?"

"I mean, people like you and me. We think we're making a difference, right? We spend our lives working inside a system that we think makes sense, but we're wasting our time, right? There's really no way for us to win. Our leaders play us for fools, and we follow along like sheep." Torrance remembered Willim Pinot's discussion about sacrifices that sometimes had to be made. He looked into Martinez's watery blue eyes and saw a fervor there that scared him. "It's funny as hell when you think about it just right."

Martinez glared with less-than-tempered impatience.

"I suppose," she said, "I should also tell you that U3 has operatives on every inhabited station around the galaxy—specifically including Europa and Mars. It would be a tragedy if a vial just like this dropped into a young woman's breakfast cereal." She paused, rolling the vial once. He caught the clear threat to Mercy and Ana. "If you have something to tell us, now would be a good time."

He set his jaw.

He had nothing to tell them they hadn't heard at the conference, but this was no longer a simple game. Sheep or no, he had to do something to stop this mission. There was no other answer. He had to disrupt the launch, and he had to destroy their communications system before Martinez could give any order in regard to his daughters.

The first step, though, was to get out of here.

He looked at the vial. It still had its injection cap.

Torrance waited until it was in mid-roll.

He lunged.

Martinez's fingers tightened, but the container slipped away, wobbling and clattering across the white tabletop.

Four hands scrabbled after it as it dropped over the edge.

It hit the floor with a solid *clink*.

Torrance leapt from his chair and grabbed it. He followed his motion, standing and wrapping an arm around Martinez's waist, pinning her against the wall. He turned the vial in his hand and put the injector to her neck. His elbows and hand ached with the pressure of his grip. The room seemed to suddenly contract.

"I want out of here," he said.

"This is a mistake, Captain."

"Let's go," he said, prodding her with his hip. "Now!"

"Where?"

He thought. There was only one place where it would make sense to launch such pods in a Star Drive ship.

"Weapons Command," he said.

———

Torrance had always heard that a man's life flashes before him when he is about to die. As they stepped toward the mess hall's doorway, the enormity of what he was doing closed in on him with the crushing weight of the ocean.

Torrance saw images of Ana and Mercy, and of fresh-faced, clear-skinned men and women marching into battle cruisers. He saw a star exploding, burning tracers of plasma spiraling into vacuum like twisted arms of jellyfish under Europan seas. He saw Alexandir Romanov, his captain from *Everguard*, and Admiral Hatch, the man in command who had never known the risk he had taken in ordering a wormhole set.

And he saw Eden, a cloud-covered planet floating in this same churning sea like a long-lost island overgrown and ugly, unworthy of second thought.

CHAPTER 18

U3 Ship *Icarus*, Alpha Centauri A System
Local Date: Unknown
Local Time: Unknown

The door of the officer's mess slid open.

The guard outside glanced over her shoulder. She was young, with dirty-blond hair and round brown eyes.

Torrance pulled Martinez closer and pushed past, holding the vial to her neck. "One step and she's dead."

The woman raised her weapon. A flash of red energy flared, and the odor of fried brains and scorched hair was everywhere at once. Martinez's body became dead weight in his arms. Torrance's gaze went to the fist-sized hole in the first officer's forehead.

The guard gave a gap-toothed grin.

She was short, with smooth muscles that showed through her uniform. Her face was set and hard, her eyes showing humor at Torrance's confusion.

"I told 'em there weren't no reason to play your game," the guard said.

Torrance dropped Martinez's body and held the vial of bionites before him like a knife. "Do you know what this is?"

"I don't really care."

"You should. These things touch you, you'll die quicker than you can pull that trigger."

The guard shrugged, but her gaze locked on the vial.

Torrance tore the lid away, then threw the open container at the guard and bolted for the corner. She grunted and jumped back. Ten meters to another corridor. Footsteps from behind. He ran, confused by a lack of traffic in the corridors. *Orion*'s hallways were always teeming.

His joints ached and his muscles were putty.

The woman was probably in shape.

In a flash of insight, Torrance understood the empty corridors. This was a suicide mission. *Icarus* was piloted by a skeleton crew—just enough to keep her flying.

A maintenance alcove loomed ahead. He stopped, entered a standard service code, and was rewarded with a control holo that spun before him. He toggled the fire retardant systems. Carbon dioxide foam hissed in the hallway. The guard's surprised yelp echoed from around the corner.

Torrance raced to the lift tubes, each of his seventy-one locals weighing like lead in his lungs.

"Central Ops," he said.

He waited.

The lift's hydraulics creaked in the silence. The sound of the guard's footsteps drew closer. She yelled something Torrance assumed was a call to whatever crew was aboard.

The lift arrived. The door opened.

Torrance stepped in.

The guard rounded the corner, her hair soaked and dripping, her gray uniform matted to her body. She raised her weapon, but the door closed before she could get off a shot.

The lift dropped.

His heart clattered in the silence. The system hummed around him.

He was defenseless. It was, he realized, a truly harrowing sensation to be completely unaware of what he would find when the doors opened.

The lift stopped, and the doors opened.

Torrance ducked in anticipation of other guards, but none were there.

Weapons Command was around the corner. The deck's power system was to the left. He could do some serious damage by playing with the power grid—maybe create a diversion that would leave him free to work the pods. The system's security, however, was tricky. If he didn't get in, the advantage of his head start would be gone.

A light flickered from atop the lift. The platform was nearing.

To hell with it.

Torrance found a service bay and accessed the lighting system. The hallway went dark. Luminescent rows of crimson emergency lights flickered on along the hallway.

The controls on the maintenance panel glowed dimly.

He followed the crimson dots to take a path to Weapons Command that wouldn't leave him exposed to the lift. He heard the door open. The air was thick. Palpable silence left him to imagine hunched guards stalking him through the hallways.

A corridor crossed just ahead of him.

It should lead to Weapons Command.

Torrance glanced around the corner and saw empty hallway.

The double doors to Weapons Command were dead ahead, but more passages opening into this one gave his pursuers plenty of opportunity for ambush. The hallway behind him was empty, too.

The guard was somewhere, though.

He had to choose. Fifty-fifty. Which way would she come?

He took a breath, turned the corner, and raced toward the double doors. By the time he neared the T, he was running at something near full speed. He stepped like a shadow across the open expanse of the hallway, then knelt in the alcove outside Weapons Command's door.

Voices came from a distance. More crew.

Trying not to breathe too hard, he pushed an entry pad.

The doors rasped open. Light spilled into the hallway darkness.

Torrance stepped in and pressed the panel on the opposite wall to close the door.

He sidled up against a barrel painted blue.

Though he had been assigned to *Orion* rather than *Icarus*, and though U3 had made a few modifications over the years, the configuration seemed comfortably familiar. It was strange to be back in this place.

He liked that it still smelled of electricity.

The barrel was cool against his fingers.

He rested his forehead on the barrel's surface to catch his breath. He was tired and sore from running. His calf muscles burned like they had been flayed.

Weapons Command lay below him, the open pit several meters down and row upon row of programmable pods stacked like cords of wood on a Wisconsin farm. The second-floor control center looked over the pit, its walls consisting of a belly-height solid wall and plasti-glass extensions that rose to the girded ceiling. Three technicians worked on a pair of wormhole pods in the pit.

Torrance counted eight tubes closed and locked.

Staggered rows of olive-coated ion torpedoes lined a distant wall. A gritty calm spread over him. He couldn't let them launch these worm-hole pods. Every torpedo had a detonation routine that could be programmed to provide a sequenced time-on-target capability. If he could detonate a few torpedoes, they would certainly destroy the bay. If he could get to the entire rack, it might well be enough to take out the entire ship.

His lips tasted of sweat and grime.

A pair of engineers hunched over a holographic display in the command center, probably loading navigation parameters into the pods. The weapons calibration station was in there.

Destroying *Icarus* here would stop U3 from planting the black hole. It was enough for him.

It had to be.

Or did it?

The shuttle bay was a short jaunt from Weapons Command.

A shuttle could never make it all the way home, and the likelihood of anyone in the United Government's structure ever coming to Alpha Centauri was nonexistent. But a shuttle was certainly capable of sending radio messages back to the Solar System, and he knew there would always be at least one person listening. Given that they were over four light-years from home, he would never live long enough for help to arrive, but at least he could make sure someone knew what had really happened.

It was as good a plan as he was going to get.

He crept toward the command center, staying out of sight of the workers below and feeling the years in his legs. He didn't have much left in him.

The door to the center was open.

"Pod nine is loaded." The voice came from the communications system—a technician relaying status from below.

"Thank you," another of the engineers said.

Nine pods loaded. The tenth would be complete soon. Assuming they had the same design parameters *Everguard* had dealt with, nine were enough to set the link. He had to move.

"How long until we go black?" the other engineer said. He was nervous. Not surprising. Torrance would be nervous, too.

"I don't know. Maybe fifteen minutes? Probably less."

"Plus flight time, right?"

"Yeah. Plus flight time."

Torrance peeked through the plastiglass.

Guidance and launch control lay directly ahead, maintenance to the left, inventory to the right. The weapons calibration station was just out of his field of view. If he could draw the engineers near, he could catch them off guard. He positioned himself at the edge of the door, then scratched quietly against the metallic edge of the frame.

Neither engineer reacted.

He scratched louder.

"What was that?" the nervous one said.

Torrance stopped.

"What's what?"

He scratched again.

"That."

The floor was tile. Footsteps drew near on the other side.

Torrance sprang forward and threw his shoulder against the closest engineer. The *whumpfh* of air leaving the man's lungs accompanied them as they fell, Torrance tangled atop the engineer.

Torrance rolled forward, stood, and caught the second engineer with a right cross that sent shivers of pain up his wrist and forearm.

The man collapsed like a sack of potatoes.

The first engineer raised to one knee, his hand rubbing the back of his neck. "What the hell are you doing?" he said to Torrance.

Torrance took two steps and kicked.

His foot struck the man's jaw and sent him spinning away.

The back of the man's head hit the corner of a desk with an ugly thud, and he fell limply to the ground.

Torrance leaned over with his hands on knees, panting. His shoulder throbbed and his foot ached. Had he broken anything? He hobbled left and right. No. He didn't think so, anyway, but suddenly all he could hear was his doctor telling him his bones were getting brittle, and that he really shouldn't be kicking younger men in the face.

He stared at the man with a surrealistic sense of the absurd.

Had he just done that? Was the man dead?

The second engineer groaned but didn't move.

Torrance went to the weapons station. It was active.

He paged through screens, his fingers shaking with adrenaline. Too long—it was taking him too long. He found the screen entry system, selected a torpedo, and set the detonation time for seven minutes. The next he set at seven, also, and the next, and the next. The work went smoothly once he had the rhythm. When he had keyed them all, he reset the system, closed the screen, and opened a security layer that locked the display against manipulation.

He started the system counter, and that was that.

The torps were programmed and armed.

It would be almost impossible to find and fix them all in time to stop him, now.

Which meant he had seven minutes to make the shuttle bay.

A footstep sounded behind him.

The area lit up in scarlet flame, and the weapons station exploded as Torrance leapt away.

The woman stood in the doorway, the same guard as before, her uniform streaked and smeared with grime, her hair dangling in short ringlets. She trained her glowing weapon on Torrance. Her eyes, dark and cold, told him her first shot was no accident. She had taken out the station to keep him from completing whatever work he had been attempting.

She was too late, of course, but she didn't know that.

A ventilation grate was mounted on the near wall. The grills were plastic, about three meters long and one high, mounted a bit off the floor.

Torrance half dived and half leapt at the duct, rolling to strike the grating with his shoulder. Plastic splintered around him. Laser ozone from her weapon cut into his nose and throat. He crashed into the duct, slipping on the dirty floor.

Pain lanced his ankle like a dagger.

Was he hit?

He crawled into the duct, scrambling on his hands and knees into the darkness like a psychotic crab. His foot burned but there was no other choice. He kept moving.

Echoes clamored from behind.

Metal ductwork screeched and popped.

The woman was following.

He was afraid then, afraid with a sensation like falling.

Torrance wanted to live.

Maybe it would be for only one additional breath, maybe for only a minute more—maybe for a mere week in a dingy shuttle floating out in space. But there in the darkness of *Icarus*'s ductwork, Torrance knew that, more than anything, he wanted to live.

His fingers slipped in the grime as he clawed his way forward.

The place smelled like oily linen.

He crashed painfully into a wall ahead, and suddenly his world was small and claustrophobic.

His ankle felt like a railroad stake had been driven through it.

Raw fear pushed him onward, but he felt the woman pursuing him, younger, fresher, and armed. His muscles screamed with every movement. His lungs seemed to collapse as he drew breath in the tiny space. He wasn't going to last much longer.

He took the left passage, thinking it the most likely to lead to the shuttle bay. A flash colored the duct crimson. The smell of hot metal brought a stifling pall to the chamber. Torrance crawled over a heavily buttressed segment of the flooring—a vacuum containment element that he realized marked the perimeter of the bay area.

A grating loomed ahead.

He threw himself into it.

It gave way, and he was falling and falling.

The ground knocked the wind out of him, and the world swam. He thought he might pass out from the pain in his foot.

Three shuttles sat in a line like massive green insects.

People raced in from the main bay entrance. Laser fire was suddenly everywhere. He crawled to take cover behind a landing strut.

The closest shuttle's ramp was open, maybe two meters away.

Gritting, Torrance launched himself toward the ramp just as something bit his thigh.

The ramp's rubber lining burned with an oily reek.

He ignored the pain and dragged himself into the shuttle.

His pants were charred and smoking.

The guard, he thought. She had shot him.

The shuttle air lock was still open. Footsteps scrabbled below. He crawled into the cockpit, sucking air against knife-sharp pain. The captain's chair was upholstered in leather. He keyed the hatch system closed.

The craft shuddered as it engaged.

Holding a nervous breath, he commanded the bay doors. They irised into six elements, dilating to expose the vacuum.

He almost cried with relief.

Rockets on. Firing. Docking release made. Yaw commands steady. Right attitude. Trimming thrusters active and warmed. He pointed the craft out the doorway and throttled the engines.

The shuttle slid forward.

Zero g took over as he left the ship's artificial gravity field and entered the umbra of *Icarus* against Alpha Centauri A. The blackness of vacuum was an open horizon in every direction. The stars glittered like pinpoints of glorious, glorious freedom.

Icarus fell away.

Torrance deployed the protective view screen against Alpha Centauri A's hard radiation.

Would he be far enough out when the torps went?

The briefest flame roared from a launch tube.

At first Torrance thought it was the torpedoes exploding, but instead a black silhouette belched from the flame, a needle-shaped figure Torrance would recognize anywhere.

A wormhole pod.

Then another and another until ten pods were flying, rocket engines engaging, turning, looping about, before taking a course toward the blazing star.

A hole formed in Torrance's gut. There's no way to win, he thought. Somehow, through the confusion and the turmoil, with both command station engineers knocked unconscious, somehow *Icarus* had launched the pods. He pounded his armrests, cursing aloud, feeling powerless and shrill.

Then the torpedoes blew.

Icarus's forefront disintegrated, fragments peeling silently from the surface, debris racing haphazardly into blackness. Flames spouted and died. Sheets of metal and composite crumpled under pressure. When it was over, *Icarus* looked like a trick cigar, one end charred and serrated, the other slim and perfect. This bird was dead, its insides gutted by pyrotechnics and vacuum.

Torrance closed his eyes.

His proximity to Alpha Centauri A obliterated the stars of deep space, but he knew they were out there.

He thought about wormhole pods.

They were away.

He had failed. They had all failed, really, hadn't they? The whole of the *Everguard* mission had caused more damage than good in the end, hadn't they?

The shielded surface of Alpha Centauri A glowed like a green fire from behind the shield. The pinprick that was one of her planets lay as the only bright point in the darkness opposite the star.

Torrance sat in the cramped shuttle pod cockpit, and thought about the black hole that would likely be set inside the star. He thought about Willim Pinot and people like him smiling, and about the carcass of *Icarus* floating freely in space, being pulled into Alpha Centauri A's gravity well. He thought about Thomas Kitchell, and Marisa, and his girls.

Yes, he thought, he had failed.

He had tried, but he was just one man and the galaxy was so goddamned big.

He felt totally alone.

CHAPTER 19

U3 Shuttle *Aurora*, Alpha Centauri A System
Local Date: Unknown
Local Time: Unknown

Torrance stripped his pants leg, cutting around areas that adhered to his burns. His thigh was darkened and goopy—radiating heat like he had been skinned, then dipped in rubbing alcohol. A small laser hole laced the fleshy place between his Achilles tendon and the bone of his ankle. He tried to prop it, but moving brought tears to his eyes. He started to pull the cloth of his pants away, but merely touching it was like razor on bone.

Finally Torrance decided merely to rest.

He gathered his senses.

It had come down to this. He was four light-years from home. The pods would make Alpha Centauri A in a few hours.

Torrance closed his eyes and remembered the last time he had been here, remembered *Everguard* and the team that had launched the original wormhole pods. The memory of his plaque came to him. The expression of faces on the return trip when Malloy blew the hull.

Funerals.

Memorials.

A chaplain extolling the virtues of a single person's contribution to the whole.

At first, that memory made him mad. One person couldn't do anything at all, could he? One person, properly motivated, could do nothing but beat his brains out on a world that was too big for him.

But a few minutes later, as his shuttle rolled and tumbled to face Eden itself, he thought about that signal. The files that had formed so much of his life.

He had one last message to send.

He toggled the radio.

"This is Ambassador Torrance Black, Captain, Interstellar Command. *Icarus* is dead," he said. He explained U3's plans for a black hole and described the flight of the wormhole pods. He warned of the threat to kill his daughters and asked for someone to look for them. He gave them his coordinates, then finished by asking whoever found this to tell Mercy and Ana he loved them. "And do the same for Oscar Pentabill," he said, remembering the man's last wishes. "Tell his wife… tell Glory…that he loved her."

He clicked off the message and set it to replay every thirty minutes, automatically casting the message upon the vacant and immense waters of the vacuum to drift in its own invisible bottle of time.

Then he lay on the captain's seat for many minutes, thinking.

Maybe someone would be close enough to hear his message and come get him.

Just the thought made him snarf.

"Fat chance, old man," he said out loud. "Stick a fork in yourself, Torrance. You are done."

What a way to go—alone inside a machine drifting about in the deepest deep space, stranded by the people he had tried so hard to serve, and unable to do a damned thing about it.

Fitting in so many ways.

He was not afraid, though, which was a strange sensation, really.

Throughout his life, he had always been afraid—afraid to be himself, worried about fitting in, afraid someone was going to walk in the door someday and see him for the fraud he so often thought he was. So he wrapped himself in cocoons whenever he could. He gave his entire life to the military, the government. Yet, now, when he had the most to lose, he wasn't afraid at all.

If anything, he was merely angry.

At one time in his life Torrance thought he might make a difference, and it turned out that he had. His command had launched the wormhole pods that brought all this on. He laughed, then. It wasn't a good laugh. Full of bitterness. Spite and regret. Maybe he had changed the world, but not for the better.

He would do so many things over again, if only he could.

He wished he had found a way to stay with Marisa, and that he had truly known his daughters. He wished he had followed the lure of the Eden files to their fullest.

That was the regret coloring his laughter.

The right thing to do had been right there in front of him the whole time, and he had always let some form of expediency stand in his way—expediency in the idea of saving his career, or in terms of doing something "more important," or "more urgent." Expediency in the name of being afraid for his professional reputation, whatever the hell that turned out to matter.

He had let all of these things take him away from the one question that mattered most.

Torrance looked out the shuttle's cockpit screen.

The planet was a pinpoint of light glimmering like a lonely beacon against the blackness of space. A finger of excitement tickled the base of his spine. His chest welled with a sensation of destiny.

Maybe it was too late.

Maybe this world was doomed one way or another.

But for the moment it didn't matter.

He stared harder into the star field and thought he saw images in the vast darkness of space.

Could he make it?

The nav panel indicated something over twelve days to get there.

He looked at his fuel monitor, his heart suddenly racing again, then twisted in the pilot seat to check the freeze-dry. He had enough fuel—barely—and enough food, and, if he skimped, enough water.

Perhaps his radio messages back home would fall on deaf ears. Perhaps he would crash on the planet and die without ever seeing another human being. But Torrance Black found that it no longer mattered.

He flipped the radio back on.

"Strike those coordinates," he said. "I'm going to Eden. I'm going to see for myself what's down there. If it's still possible, come and get me."

Then Torrance modified the shuttle's nav coordinates and commanded the engines on half power to conserve. The craft adjusted its trajectory, and Eden came into position on his navigation screen.

Exhausted, he lay back in the seat, closed his eyes, and let his body give in to the need for sleep.

If things went right, he would finally see the truth with his own eyes.

If not, he had done his best.

EPILOGUE

THE MACHINE

Esgarat
Local Date: Convergence, Year of Kax, Cycle 56
Local Time: Eldoro Low

Sitting on an isolated perch of rock that rose from the desert floor, Baraq Waganat ran his knobby fingers across the lap of his robe. The machine's sound, coming from a distance behind him, was a low hum broken by an occasional spark. Its electrical reek added to the smell of cooling dust and stone.

The open desert was a cold plane that faded into the expanse of deep darkness that came with full Convergence. The sky above was black and also cold, littered with the tiny lights that blazed without giving heat.

Little Eterdane hung over the distant horizon.

Years ago there would have been *kado* root growing here, but the nighttime was too cold for it now, and the dew that formed was acidic enough that it ate the *kado*'s delicate leaves.

Everything had changed since he was a young quadar.

There was no going back, though.

He had come to this desolate piece of desert in the remotest zones outside the Great Ring of Esgarat in order to fix the machine again.

It was a wave talker of the oldest configuration, and if Baraq was on a sudden surge of being honest with himself, he had to admit that it was nearing the end of its life. The coils had been replaced three times, an effort that grew harder to manage each day. With his father's increased paranoia, the cost of maintaining a steward full time was no longer so easy to hide. Perhaps it didn't matter, though. The machine had been broadcasting for more than two full cycles now, nearly fifty spans of Eldoro's travels, and what had it achieved?

Nothing.

Stealing the wave talker was the only thing he had known to do, and it had achieved nothing.

The idea made him shiver.

Normally, Baraq hired one of Louratna's people to do these repairs, but this time had felt different.

He closed his primaries, remembering the gauzy cover of cloud that had once protected the Quadarti.

Baraq missed his pair-mate and his son, Crissandr and Brada.

He missed the idea of hope.

Sitting here for what may well be the last time, Baraq realized how long it had been since he actually thought everything would be all right.

Tomorrow, he would return home to Crissandr, and soon after, he would see Brada.

He despaired, however, of ever seeing hope again.

———

A wind picked up, cold and harsh, making Baraq pull his robe tighter around his shoulders.

In the sky far to the south a streak of light appeared.

Interested, Baraq opened his primaries to take it in.

The light was brighter than other flashes he had seen, its color more the yellow of fire than the strobing flash of falling pebbles. It travelled more slowly as it fell, too. Its path twisted in ways that made him think of the flying machines that an old friend had once worked on.

Baraq stood up in order to get a better view, watching closely as the light faded into the darkness before touching the ground.

He raised his hand to the horizon and spread his six fingers to take a measurement.

When he was a whelpling, perhaps Baraq would have read too much into the light, but he was no longer young.

This was probably a rock. Given its burn pattern, possibly one of great value. The Family would have a use for it.

He took time to mark the positioning in his mind, and he worked to memorize his measurements—noting that the light had dissipated a handbreadth from the horizon, and mentally calculating the most likely locations for where it might have landed.

He would return with a recovery team soon.

As he worked, the wind cut into him harder and harder until, eventually, Baraq decided to return to the steward's quarters and get some much needed sleep.

The trip home, he knew, would be long.

THANK YOU!
THIS IS THE END OF STARBOUND

If you enjoyed this story, please consider stopping by your favorite online booksellers' websites to leave a review.

Word of mouth is the most powerful force in the universe when it comes to the livelihood of your favorite authors. Even a few words can help!

THE STORY CONTINUES!
FIRST YOU HAVE TO SURVIVE

Torrance Black: wounded, alone, and adrift in deep space. His tiny shuttle holds short rations and scant fuel. Ahead lies his only chance— a planet too desolate to support life. At least that's what his "experts" told him.

But someone must have sent the signals that changed his life back when he was on Everguard. Torrance believes. He's always believed.

He might die, but if he makes it to the planet he can finally learn if he was right.

But first, he has to survive.

STARCRASH, the sixth book of *Stealing the Sun*, a space based Science Fiction series from bestselling science fiction and dark fantasy author Ron Collins.

READER LIST SIGN-UP

Get copies of STARCRUISE (a stand-alone short story in the STEALING THE SUN SERIES), and Glamour of the God-Touched, volume 1 of Saga of the God-Touched Mage for Free!

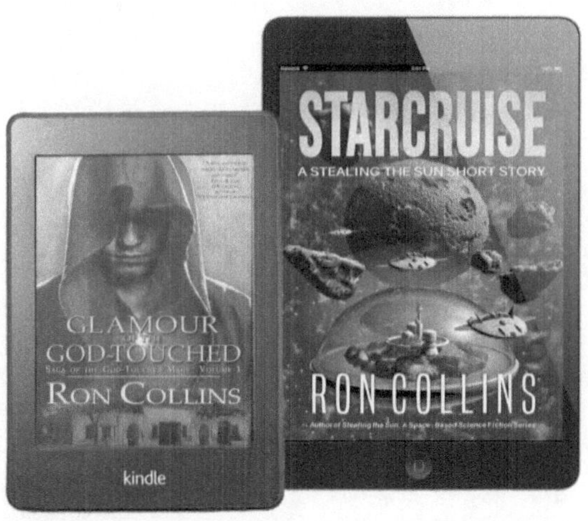

Sign-up at: https://www.typosphere.com/newsletter

ALSO BY RON COLLINS

Novels

Stealing the Sun (9 books)

Saga of the God-Touched Mage (8 books)

The PEBA Diaries (2 books)

The Knight Deception

Wakers

Poetry

Five Seven Five

(Science fictional examinations of the elusive haiku)

Collections

Collins Creek (Three Volumes)

Tomorrow in All the Worlds

Picasso's Cat & Other Stories

Five Magics

Seven Days in May (with John C. Bodin)

Nonfiction

On Writing (And Reading!) Short

(A Science Fiction Writer's Quest for Stories that Matter)

ABOUT RON COLLINS

Ron Collins is a best-selling Science Fiction and Dark Fantasy author who writes across the spectrum of speculative fiction.

His short fiction has received a Writers of the Future prize and a CompuServe HOMer Award. His short story "The White Game" was nominated for the Short Mystery Fiction Society's Derringer Award. With his daughter, Brigid Collins, he edited the anthology *Face the Strange.*

He has contributed a couple hundred or so short stories to professional publications such as *Analog, Asimov's,* and several other magazines and anthologies (including several editions of the Fiction River Anthology Series). His latest science fiction series, *Stealing the Sun,* and his fantasy series *Saga of the God-Touched Mage* are available from Skyfox publishing.

He holds a degree in Mechanical Engineering, and has worked to develop avionics systems, electronics, and information technology before chucking it all to write full-time.

facebook.com/roncollinssfwriter

twitter.com/roncollins13

instagram.com/roncollinssfwriter

bookbub.com/authors/ron-collins

goodreads.com/Ron_Collins

amazon.com/Ron-Collins/e/B00AP2IYEW

ACKNOWLEDGMENTS

As always, I need to thank my early readers, John Bodin and Sharon Bass, but the fact that this book even exists is as much due to Lisa Collins, my wife, copyeditor, and all-around wise person.